A **GOAN** ADVENTURE

Starfish Pickle

A GOAN ADVENTURE
Starfish Pickle

BINA NAYAK

Srishti
PUBLISHERS & DISTRIBUTORS

Srishti Publishers & Distributors
A unit of AJR Publishing LLP
212A, Peacock Lane
Shahpur Jat, New Delhi – 110 049
editorial@srishtipublishers.com

First published by
Srishti Publishers & Distributors in 2021

10 9 8 7 6 5 4 3 2 1

Printed and bound in India

For my father, Pandurang Pednekar.

And my daughter, Niharika Nayak.

Acknowledgement

I wrote this manuscript in 2002, in Bombay, while working at Ogilvy. I even managed to get a British literary agent, but after that, things went downhill. My life unravelled and I had to leave Bombay and move to Goa in 2003.

I kept this story aside to concentrate on pulling myself together in Goa. Among the many things I did was designing covers for Frederick Noronha's independent publishing house Goa, 1556 (I still do). I showed him my MS. He did not do fiction books then, so I kept it aside. After that, every time I made up my mind to write, I would be swamped by design assignments.

I returned to Bombay in 2009, joined The Walt Disney Company as Head of the Design Cell in 2010. Frederick and his journalist wife Pamela D'mello were always encouraging me to get my shelved book published. But I had lost steam, and now, I wasn't sure about my writing – after being exposed to some great story telling at Disney. I felt my writing was just masturbation, and didn't think anyone else should take pleasure from it.

In 2018, I was about to delete my manuscript from my computer, but decided to send it out one 'last and final' time. Anish Chandy of Labyrinth Literary Agency responded in less than fifteen minutes upon receiving my email. I'm eternally grateful to him for seeing 'something' in the MS. I had never expected to get published, leave alone get a movie deal. Thank you so very much for not giving up on me, Mr Chandy.

Thank you to Arup Bose of Srishti Publishers, Greeshma Girish, Stuti and Vini Bhati for helping with the edits.

I'm grateful to my writer partner and friend from Ogilvy – Mahinn Ali Khan. She was the first one to patiently read my nonsense. Mahinn, your writing inspires me. I hope you like how the story has shaped since you last read it. Keith and Jackie Fernandes for always supporting me, and Kaajal Majid for being my rock.

Tara's
Goa
PERNEM
KERIM
Casa de Paraiso
ARAMBOL
MANDREM
ASHVEM
MORJIM
ARABIAN SEA
SIOLIM
BARDEZ
BICHOLIM
SATTARI
SHIRGAO
CHAPORA FORT
MAPUSA
VAGATOR
PARRA
CHORAO
ANJUNA
SALIGAO
BAGA
Mae de Deus
CALANGUTE
CANDOLIM
PORVORIM
DIVAR
SINQUERIM
BETIM
AGUADA
TISWADI
MIRAMAR
PANJIM
BAMBOLIM
GMC
KUNDAIM
DONA PAULA
MANGUESHI
MPT
ANDALUSIA DISASTER
DABOLIM
MARDOL
VASCO DAGAMA
MARTINS' DREDGING
MORMUGAO
FARMAGUDI
PONDA
BOGMALO
MARGAO
BETALBATIM
COLVA
Guesthouse
BENAULIM
BAR
VARCA
SALCETE
CAVELOSSIM
MOBOR
BETUL
QUEPEM
CANCONA

VARUNA
ANDALUS

1

Flotsam Gatherer

She steps carefully over corpses covered with white sheets, as she crosses the deck of an Indian Coast Guard ship, *CGS Varuna*. Her wet suit is fused to her skin. Unzipping the front, she struggles to take it off, wondering if it's okay to undress in front of so many bodies.

What if they look? Will they see a sight worth having died for?

It's 1.30 a.m. The beep of her divers' watch mixes with the sound of her wetsuit separating rudely from her skin. It falls at her feet, retaining the contours of her body for a split second. Then, the air escapes with a soft whoosh. She stands naked; glistening with stale sweat under moonlight. Quickly donning a tracksuit, she leans over the deck railing and surveys the mess in front of her eyes.

The sea is a thick blanket, heaving with remorse. Charred remains of a Spanish merchant vessel, *MV Andalusia*, struggle to stay afloat. The temperature is a pleasant 15 degrees Celsius; comforting the corpses, slowing decomposition.

The report-for-duty call had come yesterday. All experienced divers – naval and commercial – were summoned for a search and rescue operation, fifty-five kilometres from Dona Paula, North Goa. 'Unexplained Explosion' said the SOS; a polite way of saying, 'We messed up with the dangerous cargo we were *not* supposed to be carrying.' The Coast Guard with an elite team of navy divers arrived first, and saved twelve of the fifty seamen onboard. But the ship with its cargo is beyond salvage.

The airlifted survivors – all roughly between the ages of eighteen and twenty-four – suffered 80% burns. Interred in the Vasco naval hospital, they wait for dawn and deliverance.

But wait, introductions are in order. Otherwise, you may dismiss her as a wretched creature whose only job is to hopscotch amidst lost souls.

She is a commercial diver at Martins' Dredging Private Ltd, Mormugao Port Trust (MPT). She clears the debris left behind by tankers and barges. Picking up after them as they criss-cross Mormugao Port, ferrying fertilizer, coal and iron ore. She sweeps the ocean floor, like we do our kitchen, separating hazardous garbage from the rubbish that she leaves to the sea, to vomit back at us.

She is just an ordinary sweeper; a flotsam gatherer, jetsam segregator. Was she thrown into this profession? Perhaps, due to a lack of choice.

But she has persevered for reasons best known to her. She has persevered, hoping to discover Tara, hidden somewhere in those unfathomable depths.

Does she mind the work, the cleaning, sweeping and garbage collecting? No, it is not garbage that she collects – they are treasures far beyond ordinary imagination. She watches her team gather leftovers; dismembered human body parts. Chunks of charred flesh dressed in a skin so fragile, it dissolves at the touch of lapping water.

She wonders what the dead sailors were like, when alive. Had they lived a fulfilling life, in their two-three decades of existence? Had their families loved them enough? Had they loved, enough?

How much 'enough' is enough when life is snatched from you, before your own eyes?

Roasted inside lidless sockets, those eyes now reveal nothing.

The aroma of crisping flesh awakens her stomach. Like a cookery show hostess, her glazed eyes devour the smoked and salted delicacies being served up by the ocean.

'Ladies and gentlemen, welcome to this episode of the Cookery Special on Life TV. Presenting, our first dish…

Take a once alive human being.

Skewer through lengthways. (If body is dismembered, *tikka* pieces will do.)

Marinate in ocean drawn water until rescue team is alerted.

Throw in some divers wearing shiny black rubber suits.

Lay body on ship deck or sand, and cover with white sheet to retain flavour.'

Down below, Carlos lifts an indiscernible body part, looks up at her and makes an offering. Seeing no response, he pretends to eat it. She smiles; she's not the only one missing an appetite.

Her insides are tightly wound, but on the outside, she is an ocean of calm. Relaxation techniques help divers cope with the rigours of the profession, but she prefers faster, easier methods. Opening her bag, she gropes for her little pouch, grabs a pinch-full and rolls a joint. Coaxing saliva to the tip of her tongue, she seals the butter paper and slumps against the railing, drained by the effort. Smoke swirls above, mixing with the haze hovering on the deck – a few corpses are still smouldering. Minutes later, pleasantly dazed, she pulls out her sleeping bag in a vacant spot among the columns of bodies. "Goodnight, sweet corpses," she whispers, placing her half-smoked joint into a charred, raised hand and zips herself inside her bag.

A tiny hole at the bottom of her sleeping bag nags her; it is letting the sea breeze in. Extending her big toe to seal it, she is annoyed when the hole widens to accommodate her entire toe. Waves of fatigue ebb and flow over her encased body. A heavy numbness descends, advancing millimetre by millimetre. It turns her flesh into lead, stopping abruptly at her nose. She is in a straitjacket. Fingers and toes that sometimes twitch of their own accord suddenly turn disobedient. She tries to say something – words are snatched from her mouth.

"At least say 'Taaa-raa'," she urges herself. It is her name.

Tara.

A shining star.

Tara.

Her mother named her.

Tara.

Her father cooed in her infant ears…

Somebody say that name and wake her up, quick!

'Everyone's dead,' whispers the sea breeze.

Tara hugs her sleeping bag closer, crawling deeper into its cavernous womb. A stubborn foetus refusing to be born, she clutches the umbilical cord, twisting and turning it around, trapping her own body. And yet, she cannot escape the inevitability of birth. Screaming and flailing, she hurtles towards the vaginal opening.

Exit womb. Enter vacuity.

She drifts aimlessly, leashed loosely by the umbilical cord – nylon fibre unravelling from her sleeping bag. Suddenly the cord snaps, the ocean drags her deeper and deeper, laying her down to rest on its bed.

"C'mon, Tara, breathe! Breathe!"

Something clamps tight over her nose and mouth. She yanks it off. It comes back on, tighter. She thrashes around to free herself from its clutches.

"She's having a seizure!"

Her nasal passage burns as oxygen gushes into her lungs and floods her body. Someone's stubby fingers pry open her left eye. An obstinate pupil hides behind the eyelid, revealing only the white of an eyeball.

"Tara? You okay?"

The morning sunlight is pincer-sharp. Blinking to focus, Tara recognises the face looming above hers and mumbles, "*Gengoff meeg.*"

"What?" Leaning closer, he lifts her oxygen mask to let her speak. She gets a whiff of Old Spice mixed with his coffee breath. Turning to her side, she retches copious quantities of bile.

"Better?" he asks, giving her a glass of water. "*Oi*! You scared me! I thought, what to do now? No more white sheets!"

⚓

Captain Gregory Figueiredo. Or Greg-the teller of sad jokes. The rookie naval divers guffaw obediently. But he's more impressed by the enthusiastic response from *her* team. Gregory wears his pedigree like a medal on his chest, and there are plenty of those too.

Captain Gregory Figueiredo and others like him train at elite, state-of-the-art naval academies across the country. The

Navy has recently acquired imported ROVs (Remotely Operated Vehicles) fitted with video cameras, so their divers need not venture into dangerous underwater terrain. A naval divers' life is precious, very precious indeed.

Commercial divers? Well, they are just glorified sweepers. Their naval counterparts get bravery awards – Param Vir Chakra, Maha Vir Chakra, Ashoka Chakra and so on.

Meanwhile, doing the navy's dirty work ruins the alignment of commercial divers' chakras. They fix sewage leaks, weld ships, mop oil spills and neutralise hazardous effluents in water, fully aware that there isn't an iota of heroism in these tasks. Forget ROVs and submersibles, commercial divers celebrate when their basic gear functions to the mark. Venturing underwater with their sub-standard equipment is an act of bravado, not bravery.

A doctor fusses over Tara. *Why, they even have doctors onboard!*

He declares she has the bends – decompression sickness, TYPE II – quite dangerous. It occurs when divers ascend hastily from the depths, causing a build up of nitrogen gas bubbles in their blood. But Tara is lucky. Gregory spotted her in time, choking and writhing inside her sleeping bag – seams ripped entirely on one side with the impact.

"Why didn't you recompress on surfacing?" the doctor asks her.

"No DCS symptoms," she replies haltingly, "Thought I fainted coz of hunger and no sleep."

"Fainted! You kidding me? I was there, you turned blue," Gregory interrupts.

"I would've recognised a DCS attack, definitely a type II," Tara tries to sit up. "I'll recompress now."

"Stay," the doctor orders. "Continue with oxygen for a few more minutes."

"Tara, there's so much space on the lower deck. Why sleep here?" Gregory asks. The morning breeze has ruffled some of the white sheets, revealing her sleeping companions.

"Didn't expect to fall asleep..."

"Recompress compulsorily. You didn't recognise DCS symptoms. They manifest hours after a dive, sometimes just a slight twinge in the joints and then–"

Tara interrupts, "I know, Captain. I know... had quite a few episodes in my ten-year career."

"Proud of it, *haah*?" he snaps. Turning to her team he says, "You buggers never follow safety procedures. Get the job done, damn the rules. This incident will reflect poorly on my record. *CGS Varuna* has two recompression chambers. Two, not one," he waves his fingers in the air, as if signalling a victory over the sweepers.

"Oops, I thought that was the laundromat. I mean, how else do you keep your uniforms white *na*?"

"Tara, you're taking this too lightly. The minute we dock, I'm sending you the latest edition of navy's 'Guidelines for Deep Sea and SCUBA Divers'. Out last month, bet you guys still don't have it at Martins'."

She turns to Carlos, "Do we get that?"

"Bossy says it's useless, too much space it takes. Big fat book, makes a good dumbbell though..."

Tara feels bad for Gregory. "Sorry Captain, I didn't mean to spoil your record. Should I apologize to your seniors?"

"Tara! You could've died."

"Hawww… " She bursts out laughing. "Eh, don't be hassled. It's a regular thing for us buggers!"

"Next time, use the goddamn laundromat."

"Ok!" she says, extending her hand. Gregory thinks she wants to shake and make peace. She pulls herself up, coming eye to eye with him, holding his gaze *and* his hand a little longer than necessary, feeling woozy. Carlos quickly steps in and puts his arm around her waist. Tara lets go of Gregory's hand. He walks away, stepping over the corpses without glancing down even once. Negotiating the lot, he turns to look at her, "You saw a ghost last night!"

"Aye aye Captain, you can put that in your log!"

⚓

Tara anxiously scans the skies as the *CGS Varuna* approaches Panjim. In a few minutes, colonies of seagulls will descend on the ship. Swooping on anything edible, pecking persistently to tear open the white sheets. It will be a tough task to stop them from airlifting corpse flesh. But she's extremely fond of seagulls. They're both scavengers of the ocean, keeping its waters clean. If a loved one had nestled underneath those white sheets, she would have gladly obliged to an airborne burial, or a crematory flight.

The ship docks at Panjim harbour at 7 a.m. A swarm of people strain at the barricades. Every Goan worth his *chouricos* is present. Tara dreads this kind of swamping; it is more troublesome than seagulls. The commercial divers watch from the sidelines as TV reporters mob naval divers. The Chief

Minister arrives with his entourage of cameramen and PR pundits. He promises to set up an enquiry commission.

Tara wonders what they will call it this time – *A white paper report on white-sheet-covered bodies?* The Minister for Environment gives a long speech castigating European nations for flouting rules in Third World waters, whilst maintaining impeccable standards in their own. He calls them out for dumping bad ships, bad cargo, and bad crew into poor countries. The news channels lap it up, serving it on breakfast tables of the nation.

Another assignment complete, another dive report logged, Tara looks forward to a few days of well-deserved rest.

And pickling starfish. It's time…

2

Vista do Cais

A white envelope lies unopened on Tara's dresser. It's been there since the last four days. She knows what's in it. It is always the same cursive font, as if the typesetters have run out of imagination *and* fonts.

All divers involved in Rescue & Salvage Operations of MV Andalusia, are requested to attend a memorial mass at the Church of Our Lady of Immaculate Conception, Panjim City. Time: 3.30 p.m.

Tara hates memorial masses. She does not understand the need for revisiting the calamity, recalling the agony and hopelessness – now long past. But she has protocol to follow. Wearily getting off her bed, she opens her wardrobe and fumbles through its limited contents. Her chosen line of work has made her a 'Frequent Funeraler', a reluctant collector of mortuary cards. Every piece of clothing she owns is therefore, appropriately black.

Slipping into a sombre A-line dress, she studies her reflection in the mirror and makes a mental note to keep red as the dress code for *her* memorial mass. She slumps back into bed – what else does a diver do during time off?

Rudely awakened by loud honking outside her window, Tara races to stop whoever it is before all of Saligao is rendered deaf.

"Get in!" he barks, throwing open the car door. Sheepishly, she slides into the front seat. Nalesh, Carlos and Tony are seated at the back, all of them dressed solemnly. She imagines them going to *her* memorial mass. Definitely a much nicer sight!

"May I sit at the back?"

"I'm your driver *awhat*?" asks Mr Martin Carvalho, her *Patrao*. Boss.

Old timers still call him Senhor Carvalho. An erstwhile Master Diver, his cabin walls groan with memorabilia of his glory days. Framed pictures of him with various chief ministers of Goa, certificates and letters of appreciation from the government, the Navy and clients boast of his prestige and excellence. His studio portraits show him as a dashing, sideburn-sporting young man, wearing a metal diving suit, a hard hat held stylishly by his waist. The sideburns persist even after thirty years, though very little grows in between. There's considerable growth on other fronts however, like his rapidly expanding potbelly. Martins' Dredging has just completed a successful decade of serving Goa.

Spying through the rear view mirror, Tara sees Carlos drinking furtively from a bottle of *feni,* and others, taking swigs in turns. Tony, on seeing her amused expression, gestures if she would like some.

"No," she says aloud, causing her comrades to almost jump out of the car.

"No what?" Mr Martin thunders, not taking his eyes off the road.

"No… no traffic."

The Panjim church is packed. Elbowing their way through the crowd, the tiny Martins' contingent assumes its position at the front row, beside the naval divers and coast guard personnel.

"Hello Captain Gregory!"

Preening in full naval regalia he beams at her, "Hello Madame!"

"Captain Gregory Figueiredo," Mr Martin says with a flourish. Gregory salutes him.

"I cannot thank you enough for saving my mermaid!"

Tara rolls her eyes. "Mr Martin sir, you know I hate that word! Why are female swimmers and divers called mermaids? What if I call you guys mermen?"

Mr Martin winks at Gregory, "Sorry Tara! Captain, thank you for saving my best diver."

Gregory flashes a wide grin, "My pleasure, Mr Martin."

"Good job, saving those sailors – poor chaps… and so far away from home," Mr Martin says.

"All died later that night. We did our best, but it's in god's hands."

"May god bless their souls," Mr Martin says, making a sign of the cross. "So, Gregory, will they pin another medal on your chest?"

Winking at Tara, he says, "It's broad enough to accommodate many more, no?"

Gregory blushes. "Just regular peacetime work."

Tara looks away; the sight of two grown men fawning over each other is too much for her. She wouldn't consider Gregory a good looking guy. In a diving suit, he looks muscular and short; a body builder who has mistakenly strayed in an underwater ballet. However, in a crisp white uniform, with his bulging muscles disguised, he actually looks… not bad!

"If we wear those uniforms, we'll look good too," Carlos whispers, as if reading her mind, "and by god, you'll look like Demi Moore in *A Few Good Men*. Chop your hair – like, crew cut and all."

"Shut up!" Tara says.

A large congregation has gathered for the memorial service. Sweating profusely in formal clothes and uniforms, they repeat after the Reverend Father as he valiantly paints a silver lining on the disaster.

Tara gets bored and starts day dreaming. She drifts to a quiet café overlooking the Mandovi River, and sits by its large bay windows; sipping coffee and watching tourists. Gradually, dusk descends and blinking lights dot the vast expanse of Panjim harbour. Ageing boats repurposed as floating casinos entice passersby with LED imagery. Skimpily-attired Russian girls on the gangway invite them inside; to lighten their wallets and morals. Further down, passenger ferries with misleading names like 'Paradise', 'Princessa de Goa', 'Poseidon' and 'Santa Monica' cater to the budget tourist. Their decks festooned with disco lights and ribbons, gaudily-dressed dancers show faux Portuguese dances.

"Oi Tara!" Gregory interrupts her reverie, dragging her back into church. People are filing out; the service is over. "Any plans for evening?"

"Nope, I'll just walk by the waterfront and go home," Tara responds.

"My uncle's opened a restaurant at Betim, overlooking the jetty. I promised to go today. Why don't you join me?" he asks.

"I was just..." Tara hesitates.

"Please, please. I owe you one," he requests.

"If you insist..."

"Tara, I need to say something," he pauses and smiles self consciously, "Sorry I scolded you in front of your team, regarding your DCS."

"Oh that! No big deal. I mean, everybody *sunaows* us – but you had a valid reason," she quickly corrects herself.

"What a relief, thanks!' Gregory says and goes out to get his bike. Soon after, he emerges through the crowds on his modified Royal Enfield. As they leave the church square, Tara spots Carlos near Singbal's Book House. Gregory slows down and she waves at him. He looks blankly, still clutching his feni bottle.

Vista do Cais is a cosy joint, with *azulejos* on the walls and Spanish tiles on the floor, modelled after the laid-back cafés of Lisbon. Placing an arm proprietarily around her waist, Gregory guides her inside. They walk past tables overflowing with tourists, to a wrought iron door at its far end. It leads to the kitchen.

"Oi Benny! I'm here."

A barrel-chested middle-aged man in a chef's hat looks up from a row of recently graduated trainee chefs. He steps forward eagerly.

"Tara, meet my uncle, Benny Da Costa. Benny, Tara's an old friend; she's a diver."

"*Kidhem*? Lady divers in navy? Since when? Oh boy, why I took early retirement," he says, winking at Gregory.

Tara smiles. "I'm just a commercial diver."

"Uncle Benny was the cook, I mean chef, at the INS Mandovi Mess. With twenty-five years of experience, he has opened his first restaurant."

"Lovely restaurant, Mr Da Costa."

"Thank you Tara. You're not from here, no?" he asks, with the typical contempt Goans reserve for those they consider *bhaille*, outsiders.

"I grew up in Bombay. Ten years ago, after mom died, dad and I returned to our ancestral home in Saligao."

"*Awois!* The *Bomoicaan* is now a *Goemcaan*. Welcome-welcome," he says enthusiastically. "Sorry about your mother."

"Oh, it was so long ago…"

Benny continues, "You see, Tara, all this is disappearing," he points to the tables and the tourists eating leisurely. "*Phinish!* Now all Café Coffee Days and KFCs. They say in big letters 'Self Service'. Nonsense! I sit at home no? Serve myself all I want… why pay good money for that, haan? That's why I open this restaurant. Sit as long as you want. Eat, don't eat, doesn't matter. Be happy!"

He directs them to the garden behind his café. It has a small patch of spice plants and herbs. Basil, dill, lemon grass and Portuguese chillies, blend with end of February warmth, injecting the air with a fragrance at once tangy and piquant.

Air good enough to eat, except, she cannot survive on love and piquant air.

Bougainvilleas spill through balusters of a whitewashed compound wall. Jackfruit and mango trees near the perimeter are decorated with lights. Paper lanterns with little squares cut out, drop from their branches. Swaying with the breeze, they launch thousands of light patterns into orbit. Like tiny incandescent whirling dervishes.

Two chairs and a table of white cane sit in the midst of it all, covered with the ubiquitous red and white checked tablecloth. Da Costa has already served the special – freshly-baked bread rolls, Chicken Cafreal, Garlic butter Calamari, and butter-fried tiger prawns wrapped in bacon.

"So much food!" Tara remarks as they sit down.

"Eat all you want. It's free," Gregory says enthusiastically.

"You eat all *you* want; I eat light at night. Now don't lecture me on the nutritional needs of a diver, ok?"

"Tara, why you treat me like this? I'm not some lecturer from Dhempe College," he asks in a mock plaintive tone.

"But you *do* lecture all the time."

"I'm just used to giving orders, you know. Anyway, how are Dad and Aajji?"

"Both fine. That reminds me, haven't told them I'll be late. Dad still worries. I mean, I've been in Goa ten years now…" saying this, Tara sends a message from her mobile.

"Wait – *ten* years? You mean we first met ten years ago, at the trials? Wow! And look at you! Ms Tara Salgaonkar, you survived Goa! "

"Deserve a medal, no?" Tara smiles.

"Here, take mine!" He winks. "Seriously, I didn't think you'd last so long. I mean, Goa's hardly challenging for a naval or commercial diver. Bombay and Cochin is where the real action is. That's why I spent my first five years in Cochin. But you,

you've only worked here, at Martins'. Tara, will you leave if you get a better opportunity?"

"Not sure if I can fit in anywhere else. You see, Goa has ruined me," Tara replies

"What! I can't believe you're saying this. At one time you didn't fit in. Look at you now!"

Just then, Benny Da Costa appears with more specials.

"Oi Benny! Join us. Listen to some funny stories of Tara when she was new to Goa."

Benny pulls a chair and sits down. Which Goan does not enjoy a bout of gossip?

Gregory starts, "Exactly ten years ago we were all waiting outside INS Mandovi…"

"Okay! Worst comes first, haan?"

"Why Tara, don't you like talking about your training period? Wish those days would never end."

"*You* had a training period; I dived into work from day one."

"Ok-Ok, let Tara tell her story, Gregory," Benny says impatiently, "I've to get back to the kitchen."

3

Fresh off the Boat

Tara starts hesitantly, "Ten years ago I arrived in Goa, fresh off the boat from Bombay." She has recounted this story differently for different people.

"Well, not actually, as the Konkan Sevak and Konkan Shakti steamer services from *Bhaucha Dhakka* had been stopped".

"They were pulled into service by the Indian Navy for the Srilankan LTTE fiasco," Benny tell Tara. She nods knowingly.

"My first day in Goa I saw an ad in the newspaper by the Naval Academy, for their deep-sea divers' training programme. Selected candidates would be sent to Cochin, to INS Venduruthy for further training."

"I had inside information about this, from Benny!" Gregory says triumphantly. "I didn't wait for the ad. I had started preparing much ahead."

Nepotism. Tara glares at Gregory. "Oh sorry, please continue," he responds.

"They mainly wanted naval cadets, but civilians with marine and mechanical engineering degrees could apply too. So I applied. I was a marine engineer from Bombay, a batch-topper, and I was the National and State champion in swimming – 100 metres Freestyle and Butterfly. I thought I would definitely get in through the sportspersons' quota." Tara gets pensive. Benny eggs her on, one eye on his kitchen.

"Yes, so I stood patiently outside the gates of INS Mandovi. Seeing no activity, I went inside, walking towards the swimming pool. Two guards stopped me. An officer asked if I was looking for someone. 'I'm here for the trials,' I replied. 'Sorry, no women,' he laughed."

"Luckily, I had carried a newspaper clipping of the advertisement. I showed it to him, and told him that there was no mention of gender. He replied it was a mistake on their part, but everybody knew that the Indian Navy only recruited male divers."

"You know, they charge by the word for recruitment ads in newspapers. That PRO was just trying to save money I think, by not stating the obvious," says Gregory.

Tara rolls her eyes.

"And then?" asks Benny.

"Then I threatened to sue them for misleading people."

"What! Sue the Indian Navy?" laughs Benny.

"Ya, but I agreed not to if they let me try out. I had travelled all the way from Bombay only for the trials, I told them."

"That incident is now part of academy folklore," Gregory tells Benny. "And you know what, my batch is referred to as 'Tara's batch'. Unofficially, of course."

"Someone told me… I thought he was joking," laughs Tara.

"How could we have recruited her, Benny? The Indian Navy is not ready for women divers, even from the best maritime institutes in the world."

Benny smiles sympathetically at Tara, "Abroad, ladies do all things gents do. Abroad, ladies are posted on submarines also. *Ai Saibini!*[1] But, this is India. Then what happened?"

"Made a fool of myself," mutters Tara.

"You know how it is at recruitments na? Half the people can't swim a 50 metre lap. What a bloody fish she was – still is. We were all drooling, imagining a woman in our batch!" looking at Tara, Gregory says, "When you ran out crying bitterly, all of us felt like crying too!"

"I didn't cry bitterly, just cried for two seconds maybe. Rushed home on my Kinetic and this damn old man darted in my path, thank god I braked in time. That Verem slope is so steep man!"

"Maybe you didn't see him because you were crying?" Gregory says jokingly.

Tara looks irritated, "Anyway, as I was saying, thanks to you guys, I got my Martins' job. Those geriatric officers recommended me to Mr Martin. Something good *did* come from that embarrassing episode."

"Navy's loss was commercial diving's gain," says Gregory.

"Absolutely!" says Benny, "I'll finish up in the kitchen and come back. Wait, ok?"

Gregory nods at him. "I'll drop you home if it gets late," he says to Tara.

"Thanks! And, to answer your earlier question, about leaving Martins' for a better job… don't think so,"

"Why not?" he asks.

"I'm happy at Martins'," she replies.

---

1. Mother Mary

"Tara, there are better dredging companies in Goa."

"Maybe there are, so what?"

"Martins' has a reputation for undercutting. See, clients don't mind paying for specialised work. But for common jobs, they favour the lowest bidder. You guys get all the common jobs."

"So I risk my life for common jobs? All my DCS episodes for common jobs?"

Gregory avoids answering her. "Your boss is a desperate bugger."

"He pays us well, and on time," she replies bluntly.

"Why you support him? He's not letting you grow. Lesser people have gone far ahead of you."

"I had no idea a competition was on. And, for what? To see who dives deeper and dies harder?"

"Ok, forget I said that. Martins' has a bad safety record, you know it. Not good in the long run, especially for a woman. Join a firm with a better safety record. People will grab you like this," he snaps his fingers.

"Ha, they'll grab my team – they'll even grab lousy Carlos, but not me! I'm stuck at Martins'. If I quit, I'll end up in the *ranchikood*[2]."

"The Bindass Bombay babe's gone all soft *awhat*?"

"Not fair, Gregory! All these years you teased me coz I didn't fit in, and now that I do, that's no good either."

"Tara, you're still tinkering with sewage leaks and scrubbing barges. You know, one day – and that day is not far – you'll b scrubbing some rusted barge, you'll look down at your hands

---

2. Kitchen (Konkani)

crisscrossed with cuts, and wish you were somewhere else. But it'll be too late, I'm telling you!"

"Wow, you saw my future! *Chal*, let's get you a stall at the Saturday Night Market. Leave the navy and sit with a crystal ball."

"Tara, I'm not joking. At least give it a thought."

"Tell you what, Gregory, when the navy is ready to recruit women divers, call me. We'll do a repeat of the INS Mandovi incident. Who knows, you'll be the geriatric officer recruiting a geriatric me! Imagine me in a swimsuit at sixty or seventy!"

He laughs uncontrollably, "Not that long. Actually – and this is inside information – it may happen in two-three years."

"What!"

"I said, *maybe*. Don't tell anybody, ok?"

"You're lying!"

"Swear!"

Tara becomes pensive. "Now that you mention it, strangely, I feel nothing. Forget two-three years, if the navy asks me now, I'll say no. Can't imagine working anywhere else but Martins'."

"What can I say, Tara. Certainly good for Martins', though I don't think they deserve you. Anyway, enough of this talk, what else you been up to?"

"Not much. In a few days, I'll be back at work. Same old-same old. And you?"

"I'm due for a posting in Bombay or Cochin, just three months. Dreading it actually. I hate Bombay," Gregory says.

"You're not from Bombay, Gregory. You're not allowed to hate her."

"Only you have that privilege *wot!* That city's an open gutter."

"Don't exaggerate, okay!" Tara says.

"I'm not! The sea's choking. Even your MSAAA has discontinued its Sunk Rock to Gateway Sea Race…"

Her eyes light up. "So long since I competed, but hey, it's stopped temporarily for security reasons."

"That, and pollution."

"There's no place like Bombay," she insists.

"Dead city," he taunts her.

"Perfect! I'm a dead body gatherer from a dead city," Tara says.

"Scurry like rats to work on one end of the island. Scurry back at night to matchbox-sized houses on other end… that's all you Bombayites know."

Tara smiles. Had this conversation taken place a few years ago, she would have bitten his head off. Like most Goans, Gregory is incapable of understanding the essence of a Bombayite's life; work is worship, time is precious, and money is the only god. So, she feeds him what he wants to hear. "Don't ask me, I've sold out to your Goan way of life."

There are things that Tara has only recently understood. What appears as sloth in Goans is actually their evolved understanding of life, that it is predestined. So they go through its motions at a relaxed pace. However, this understanding works only in Goa. Maybe the balmy weather has something to do with it. Or, that smelly brew, feni. In her early years in Goa, not only was she stubborn, but she also hated feni. She resisted all things Goan to appease her Bombay ego.

But, like waves crashing against rocks at Anjuna, disintegrating them into tiny pebbles, Goa ground her down.

Gregory consults his watch. "Shit, we've been yapping for more than three hours!" he exclaims. "Benny fell asleep in the kitchen, I think. Let's leave."

"Take the Betim-Pilerne road. It goes straight through my village," Tara suggests as they head out.

"That's a bad road to take at this hour. Too many sharp turns, and it's very steep."

"Afraid of ghosts *wot*?"

"Ha! My old Bullet won't be able to handle it. I'm taking the highway, okay?"

The NH-17 is quite deserted, except for an occasional outstation truck and Gregory's bike. Tara shivers as a blast of cool breeze hits her. Gregory is insulated by his leather jacket. She holds him tight, stealing some of his warmth.

"We make a crazy pair, don't we? You're a white knight, I'm a dark one." The breeze plucks her words and jumbles them like jigsaw pieces.

"Dark what?"

"Dark knight."

"Ya, streetlights knocked out here too…"

Reluctantly they distance their bodies on arrival at her house. Tara wants to hold on a little longer. "Come in," she says, "I'll show you my coral collection." Saying it quite nonchalantly, as only she can, without the fluttering of eyelashes or pouting of lips. He agrees.

Her home is her dark kingdom.

She prefers it that way. Barely visible due to thick foliage, it is a guest house to the main ancestral house – both built more than a century ago by her paternal great-grandfather, Shankarao Salgaonkar.

The main ancestral house adheres to principles of *vaastu* and is inward looking, while the guest house is in the Indo-

Iberian style. A wild gourd creeper bearing bright yellow flowers erratically overruns the red-tiled roof. In its centre is a small open courtyard. The two houses stand a hundred metres apart, the distance bridged by orchards of mango and jackfruit. Tara's dad and her *Aajji*[3] reside in the main house.

Tara had lived with her folks in the main house for a brief period of two months, till she got the Martins' job. Then her erratic work schedule started interfering with Aajji's sleep, giving her bouts of acidity. Tara considered renting an apartment near her workplace in Vasco, or living in a women's hostel, but Aajji would hear none of it.

"A young, unmarried girl must stay with her family, or people will talk," she insisted. So Tara moved into the guest house.

Locked for over three decades, their guest house was used by outstation relatives and friends who came to meet them. Those relatives and friends now preferred checking into cheap 2-star hotels and Airbnbs sprouting like paddy in monsoon all over the Goan countryside. So, it remained deserted for a long time until Tara moved in and made it habitable once again.

Living in it gives her the isolation she craves. The orchards cut her off visibly and literally from the outside world. The guest house has moulded her with its sparse sensibilities. Tara lives and behaves like a tenant, making no alterations, hammering no nails in the walls, keeping her possessions at a bare minimum. She pays a hefty rent that slowly depletes her mental balance – her recurring nightmares – the occupational hazards of a rescue diver handling corpses for a living.

---

3. Grandmother

Over the years, Tara has learnt to circumvent the nightmares. She stays up late and sleeps at dawn. Or she goes to bed only when she is dead tired. Yet, every night is a fight.

Because, with sleep comes Morpheus, forcing her to worship at his altar – demanding his pound of brain flesh.

Rent, for an unseen but ever present landlord.

As Gregory steps into the house, his uneasiness is palpable. After ten years of being acquainted, and five years of working together occasionally, Tara has invited him to her place. He wonders if it's because of their shared experience of a disaster. As they say, tragedy brings people closer. Besides, he saved her life, so she must be grateful no!

"So many trees! Chop off some. So dark in here. You'll need lights on during daytime."

"I'm not home during daytime, and it's dad's orchard. He'll chop me into pickle-sized pieces if I break even a twig by mistake."

She continues walking, leading him to the courtyard. It's the only area where light peeps in, being open to the sky. The full moon has washed it to a square of blinding white. Gregory adjusts his eyes.

Tara points at two easy chairs in the centre of the courtyard, "Sit, I'll fix you a drink. Aajji doesn't like me drinking, so I only keep vodkas and clear rums. She thinks it's water! Will Vodka with Sprite do?"

"Plain Sprite, please," Gregory says, surveying her rooms while she walks to the kitchen.

"You have a room full of aquariums," he remarks, when she returns with drinks, "Side business awhat?"

Tara smiles. "I love aquariums; they help me relax. I can spend hours watching fish."

He immediately perks up. "I have a gold fish bowl in my bedroom."

"Children keep goldfish." Tara chuckles.

"Oi! Don't show off! So where are your famous corals?"

"In those aquariums. I steal them during my dives and grow them in there, they're alive," she says. "Perfect environment for my marine fish."

"Is that allowed?"

"C'mon, I'm not a coral black marketer. Just few for my fish tanks. By the way, you get them at all fish 'n' pet stores in Panjim. They come illegally via Bangkok and cost a bomb."

"Tara, if all divers collect corals for their fish tanks, my god, there'll be no reefs left."

"So arrest me!" she says, pointing her closed wrists to him. He holds them.

"Can I drink while the handcuffs are on?" she asks. Gregory quickly lets go.

"So, are you going to show them?" Gregory asks.

"Still interested in my illegal activity? Okay, come."

Tara walks to her bedroom and stops at the door, "Look inside while I get a refill." He grabs her waist as she turns to leave, pulling her close. She quickly reduces his crisp white uniform to a crumpled heap, his important medals – loose change on the floor. Pinned against her bed, Gregory is unusually quiet.

"What? Don't like woman superior?" Tara asks.

"Ummm..."

Ah ... a missionary man.

Non-experimental.

Naval diver!

They switch positions, she servile, he superior. He thrusts with a Jesuit's zeal. She feels a familiar tingling sensation creeping under her skin, "I... can't... breathe..."

"Huh?"

She comes up for air. "Yes!"

Halleluiah!

"Were you fair before you started diving?" he asks. She laughs at his choice of subject for post-coital conversation.

"We lived beside Versova Beach in Bombay. Then I started living at the swimming pool. Don't remember my original colour."

She extends an arm to observe. "Aajji says no one will marry me. They should ban those Fair & Lovely ads on TV, no?"

Gregory yawns and disengages. He retrieves his stuff from the floor. What follows next is the closest Tara has ever come to experiencing a religious ritual. With great reverence, he smoothes the creases on his uniform, folds it neatly and places it on a chair. Next, he picks up his medals. Spitting into his handkerchief, he wipes each one till he is satisfied with the shine, and places them over his uniform. Stepping back, he admires his handiwork. Tara looks away, not wanting to be caught staring.

"Tara, get me some water."

"Kitchen's to your left. Help yourself."

He inspects her aquariums on the way out, stops and guffaws. "Tara keeps *Tarafish*."

Her kitchen is spartan, its wooden shelves devoid of utensils. She uses it to make coffee and boil an occasional egg or two. Gregory opens her mini refrigerator and drinks directly from a bottle. He surveys the musty room. Two ceramic pickle jars stand at the far end of an L-shaped platform, their lids sealed with cheesecloth.

Startled by a sudden craving, he shivers as it cloaks his entire body with goose bumps of memories. Rummaging through drawers of a cabinet, he hunts for a spoon. He's about to pull off the cheesecloth and pry open the lid.

"Don't," she growls in a low voice.

Gregory almost drops the jar, and jumps out of his naked skin.

"A little taste?" he asks sheepishly, as if caught with his fly open.

"No!" she wears her nakedness like a steel armour.

"But it's a clean spoon."

"Just mixed it yesterday. It'll spoil if you open."

He returns the jar to its place but continues eyeing it.

4

Pickling Season

"You want me to cut so many mangoes? Are you taking pickle orders from local shops again, Aajji?"

"Just ten *bharnis*[4], Tara. Four for us and the rest for your cousins and aunts," Aajji says with a smile. She is always beaming with joy when she is making pickle.

"It's my time off! I need rest," Tara says in an irritated tone.

"Who's making you work? Here, apply coconut oil on your palms and start."

Mid-February to mid-March is pickling season in the Salgaonkar family. In their orchard, three trees provide raw mangoes for pickling – *'Ghotts'*. The rest are Alphonsos and Mancurads, for export.

Five years ago Aajji had concocted a new pickle masala; it was a big hit in the village, with people queuing at their door. That year's pickle batch ran out by October and Aajji was forced to buy

4. Ceramic pickle jar (Konkani)

readymade pickle from the supermarket – blasphemy for a family that owned a mango orchard. And such synthetic tasting pickles they were. That year Aajji decided to get into the pickle business.

It seemed like a great idea at first. Tara's dad was quite pleased, considering it a natural progression of their core business. But, there was a small hitch. Aajji's plan was entirely dependent on Tara quitting Martins' and joining her.

Tara was a good pickler, and an even better cutter, dicing raw mangoes into perfect wedges, equal to the last millimetre. Apparently, this was a Salgaonkar woman's speciality. After all, the secret to a good raw mango pickle lay in the cutting of mangoes.

Tara had inherited the skill and mastered it. But making it her life's work? Not really! She had other plans.

"Aajji, why can't we eat readymade pickle like normal people? It's not so bad. I quite like the taste of some brands. There's a tanginess we can't seem to replicate..."

"My dear, that's synthetic vinegar. It's a short cut. Sea salt is the best preservative. And, what we get from the Arpora *agaarwaado*[5] is the best in Goa."

"But the pickle takes so long to get ready," Tara protests.

"Isn't waiting the best part? Think about it, Tara," says Aajji, mixing the spices with bare hands.

"We come from the sea. It touches our lives in every way – gives us fish, salt to preserve pickles and food. It touches you

---

5. Salt pan

every day, coats you with its flavour. You know, Tara, you'll live long. Seawater is good for health. Look at me, I'm nearly ninety."

"Why Aajji, were you also a diver like me?"

"I loved swimming in the sea. I was good. Maybe as good as you. You don't get it from your dad; he's a land guy. He speaks to the soil, like his father."

"But we Salgaonkar women speak to the sea," says Tara, cutting the last mango and depositing it in the brine filled jar. "That reminds me, got to call office for my schedule. Can't believe, two weeks passed so quickly."

"Tara, if you hate going to office..."

"Why don't I quit and become your assistant? No Aajji, I'll continue my dialogue with the sea."

"Someday you'll come around." Aajji smiles.

"Maybe! And I'll make the best pickle in the world. You'll be proud of me. But not yet, Aajji."

"Hope I'm alive to see that day."

"Oh, you will, Aajji. Sea salt is the best preservative."

5

An Odd Fish

Martins' Dredging Pvt. Ltd. is centrally located at Mormugao Port Trust. The Port Trust authorities rely on them to do their

dirty work – cleaning oil spills, patch-up and repair jobs on docked cargo ships, and retrieving decomposed, drowned bodies. Martins' employees are mainly divers, clerical staff and a few secretaries.

Every year a picnic is organised, with the sole purpose of getting the office staff to mingle, as much as they hate it. It's a family affair with wives, husbands and kids, typically scheduled for March-end or early April – whenever the school term ends. This year, however, Mr Martin has pulled it forward to February-end, so his divers can take a day off while they recover from the Andalusia operation – their biggest and most challenging search and rescue till date.

When a circular is sent out, only six people sign; all of them divers. The secretaries sarcastically refer to it as a 'Divers only' picnic. But one diver has also opted out – Tara Salgaonkar.

Mr Martin wonders why Tara has opted out. He summons her to his cabin.

"Why aren't you coming for the picnic? No secretaries this time. Perfect for you."

"I'm cleaning my fish tanks, Mr Martin."

"*Ai Saibini*, that's the lamest excuse I've heard all day."

"Swear on *Saibin mai*, I really have to. Couldn't do it during time off."

"How long does it take to clean a fish tank? Do it on Sunday. Come for the picnic, Tara."

"It's not *a* fish tank, Mr Martin. I have nine. Largest is ten feet. All custom made. I collect exotic and rare starfish."

"Really? You know, I used to collect corals! Long ago when it was legal and I was a diver." he chuckles and continues.

"Amazing coral collection I had. All gone! Friends and relatives stole it."

The colour drains from her face. "I'm not coming, and please Mr Martin, don't send another circular saying it's compulsory. Cut my salary if you want."

Mr Martin is offended. "Why would I cut your salary? You don't want to come, don't come."

Amongst his divers, Tara is the odd fish. She speaks her mind without worrying about the consequences. Her bluntness is often misconstrued as rudeness. Only when you spend enough time with her, do you realise that she's slightly deficient in the empathy department. A senior diver, she's as good as he was at her age, perhaps better.

Ten years ago, Mr. Martin did not imagine that she would last this long. Times were different then; nobody employed women divers – there weren't any. So when Tara came to meet him, he grabbed her. She had reference letters from the recruiting officers at INS Mandovi.

Martins' Dredging was new and looking for outsourced jobs from the navy. In any case, he had reasoned then, having a lady diver on the team would be a good thing. It would enhance his firm's image, making it a pioneer in recruiting the fairer sex for commercial diving. No complex or hazardous jobs would be assigned to her, just simple clean-up operations. Which his male divers hated anyway; they complained that it was a maid servant's job.

Besides, what did they say about Bombay girls? They all looked like Bollywood heroines. But, Tara could, at best, pass off as a dance extra. She could be relegated to the last rows of item song sequences, never in front. But even that would suffice to boost the morale of his jaded male divers, motivating them to come to work every day. So, he recruited Tara to be the office eye candy.

Eye candy? More like a knitting needle in the eye!

Mobor beach in South Goa is the chosen picnic spot. Given the reduced attendance this year, Mr Martin relaxes the rules, allowing divers to get their girlfriends. They will squeeze inside two cars – his Pajero and Carlos' Fiat.

Panjim Kadamba bus stand is the meeting point, being adjacent to the Margao road. Everyone will assemble there at 7.30 a.m. sharp on Saturday morning.

As the other divers are discussing picnic plans, Tara walks into the divers' room. From the corner of an eye she sees Carlos observing her. "*Bai*[6], not coming this year also?" he asks, standing right behind her. "You haven't attended a single office picnic in ten years!"

"Wrong! I have attended one in the year that I joined. That's the reason I don't attend anymore."

Carlos looks exasperated. "But no *secys* this year *ya*! Just us, divers."

"If I don't clean my tanks, my starfish will die. The sea water tanker has already been called."

"Tell them to come on Sunday."

---

6. A Konkani term of endearment for girls and women, equivalent to 'dear'.

"Can't! And enough of this stupid picnic, it's all everybody's talking about. Listen, Aajji was asking for you. She's making *Khatkhatem*[7] for dinner tonight. Come, ok?"

"Don't feel like eating Khatkhatem, Tara."

"I'll tell Aajji. Nice pasting you'll get next time you come… Bye, see you after the picnic. Have a nice one."

"Bai, wait! Can I take some home?"

"How much you want? Full week's supply? I'll tell her." They leave office at 8.30 p.m. When they reach Saligao after an hour, there's a power cut. Carlos parks his car in her orchard. "I'll go tell Aajji to pack the extra Khatkhatem. Are we eating with family in the main house?"

"Do you want to?"

Carlos ponders for a minute, "No, let's eat in your house. I'll just say hi and come."

"Don't chit-chat too long with the old woman."

After a few minutes Carlos returns, followed by the maid carrying two casseroles and an emergency light. She gets plates from the kitchen and serves them dinner. Carlos and Tara eat in silence in the dim light. Afterwards, they go to the courtyard; a *chattai* is spread out in the middle. Tara gets some pillows from her bedroom and they sprawl comfortably side by side. She hands him one earphone of her iPod. He waves it away. The power cut has muzzled village televisions that blare dinnertime serials at this hour.

"Bai, I think there are extra stars *only* above your courtyard…"

---

7. Vegetables in coconut gravy spiced with *terphalam* (a variety of pepper)

"Ya, they all come and crowd up there, to watch me," she says, pointing to the patch of star-infested sky enclosed by her courtyard.

"Bai, you know Mr Martin has allowed girlfriends for the picnic?"

"I heard. Another reason I can't come. No girlfriends!" she says triumphantly.

"Stupid, you're supposed to get a boyfriend."

"Don't have one," Tara says in a matter-of-fact tone.

"But I see you at cafes with Navy boy Gregory."

She raises an eyebrow. "Are you keeping tabs on me? He's just a friend, ok? Don't go all big brother on me."

"Arrey, I meant to say you can invite him."

She narrows her eyes, "Really? I know what you're doing. Trying to find out if something's going on."

"*Ai Saiba*, you take everything the wrong way, Tara!"

"Mr Martin will never allow a navy diver to our picnic. But forget that, I hate picnics – with or without boyfriends. Nothing and nobody can drag me to one."

Carlos shifts a little, forming a gap between their bodies. "I'm going home."

"So soon? You're upset!"

Tara gets up and sits on her haunches, holding her ears. "So sorry, Carlos, I won't call you big brother again," and bursts out laughing seeing his expression. Both break into giggles as she climbs over him and pins him to the *chattai*.

Carlos envies the stars above who watch over her. For now, he is grateful to be allowed so close.

6

Lost Lisa

There are eight people at the Panjim Kadamba Bus Stand. Mr Martin was expecting twelve. Only Nalesh and Carlos are accompanied by their girlfriends. He finds it hard to believe his dapper divers are incapable of finding dates. Hopefully, it has nothing to do with the long hours they keep at work.

Nalesh's girlfriend, Rani, is a journalist with a leading local daily. They hooked up when she did a story on one of their search ops. Carlos' girl, Lisa, does not look a day older than sixteen. Mr Martin pulls him aside and enquires if he's taken permission from her parents.

"What permission? Boss, she's an adult."

Parking their cars in a shady coconut grove, they hit the sea first, the boys wearing fluorescent swimming trunks that hurt the eyes. It's a pleasant change from wearing dark wetsuits and entering it to work. Everything is perfect till mid-afternoon, and then a small argument erupts between Lisa and Carlos.

Lisa's been sitting by the shore all morning, watching others swim. Every few minutes, one of the boys goes ashore and cajoles her to join them, without success. She throws a tantrum, "Carlos, I want to go home. I'm bored."

Carlos is lying in ankle deep water, surrounded by bottles of beer and feni. "Join us baby. C'mon, it's safe. No currents."

"I don't swim," Lisa says.

"You don't want to swim, or you don't know how, Lisa?"

"Both."

Carlos looks puzzled. "You were buying swimsuits at the shop where I met you."

"So? Only swimmers can wear them?" Lisa is getting irritated now.

"No! But I thought you were a swimmer," says Carlos, shaking his head and laughing.

"Let's go no!"

"Go where? We just got here! Chillax baby, make a sand castle or something."

Lisa gets up. "I'm going for a walk."

"Fine, don't go too far." Carlos says and leaves her alone.

⚓

At 5.30 p.m., Rani wakes up and quickly folds her beach mat. "Eh Nalesh, wake up! Lisa's not back yet," she says, shaking him. "Go wake that Carlos, tell him to call her."

"My mobile's in my car," Carlos mutters, his eyes barely open. Wearily, he gets up and walks to his car. Opens the door and face palms. "She left her handbag and mobile in my car! Now what?"

"We search. Bloody hell, no break on a picnic also…" Nalesh mutters.

"Don't look in water. She won't go there, can't swim," Carlos tells Nalesh and flops back on his mat.

"Arrey, aren't you coming?" Nalesh asks Carlos. "She's your responsibility!"

"Must've gone home," Carlos says.

"How? Her handbag's in your car," Nalesh asks.

"Anyone will give her a lift, with that red swimsuit she's wearing. Full on, men! Full on!" Carlos laughs.

Rani slaps him. "I pray she hasn't done that. Forgot what happened here last year?

"What?" Carlos asks, shocked by Rani's slap.

"A bunch of college kids…" Mr Martin says to Carlos, "and…"

"Their bodies were found mutilated in the bushes," Nalesh completes the sentence.

They quickly form two groups, one scanning the village, the other, the beach. After two hours of futile searching, they gather around in a tight huddle to deliberate their next move.

"*Patrao,* should we go to office, get searchlights and diving equipment, just in case?" asks Nalesh.

"Was about to suggest that," Mr Martin says. "Let's prepare for the worst. Lisa may have drowned. We'll have to inform her parents first, then file a missing complaint. Come Carlos, you talk to her parents while we drive to the police station."

"Wait! I don't know them. Don't have their number," says Carlos.

"Go through her mobile and find it."

"Should we call Tara?" asks Nalesh, glaring at Carlos, who is busy going through Lisa's contact list. He looks up on hearing Tara's name. "Don't give me those looks man."

"No point calling Tara," Mr Martin tells Nalesh. "Let Carlos call Lisa's parents and check if she's home. No wait, Carlos! You don't call. Let Rani call. Better if a girl calls."

Carlos looks relieved. He reads out a number from Lisa's contact list to Rani, "Her mom's number. There doesn't seem to be a dad – at least no number."

"What should I say?" asks Rani.

Mr Martin answers, "Ask for Lisa. If they say she's not home, say Lisa forgot her mobile with you. Also, leave your number. Tell them to call you the moment she's home."

"But Patrao, if we involve cops, they'll inform her family. Land up at her house," says Nalesh.

"We have to involve cops. Nobody did this on purpose. Bad things happen..." Saying this, Mr Martin drags Carlos by the collar to his Pajero. Turning around he says, "Oh, one more thing. If we need a full-fledged search operation, costs will be deducted from everybody's next month's salary."

Driving down the pitch-dark road, Mr Martin starts worrying about Lisa for the first time. This is unlike regular search operations, where there are bodies to be fished out. This is someone he knows – not just a body. He worries what people will say; he can already see the headlines in tomorrow's papers – 'Young girl goes to picnic with the best rescue divers in Goa. And drowns.'

"What will Tara say when she gets to know?" mutters Carlos. He's been quiet all along. "Damn! She'll hold this against me for years."

"Carlos, forget what Tara will say, worry about Lisa's parents. How will you face them?"

There's not a soul on the road, even though it's only 9.30 p.m. Driving at full speed, as if on autopilot, Mr Martin is aware that he should look out for dogs and small animals scurrying in their path. But nobody is out tonight.

Suddenly, as he navigates a sharp turn, he sees a pair of hitchhikers waving at his car. Probably villagers going to the city, covered in thick woollen blankets. The nights on Mobor Peninsula get quite cold.

"Don't stop, we'll get late," says Carlos. "Look at them, so filthy."

Mr Martin speeds past, watching the pair shrink in the rear view mirror, still within the trajectory of his car's rear lamps. The shorter one squats on the road, holding his head in a dejected manner. The blanket slips, revealing a flash of red. Seconds later, darkness swallows them. He slams hard on the brakes and reverses the car at full throttle.

"I thought we weren't going to give them a lift… "

"My group, they came for me!" she shouts, recognising Mr Martin and Carlos. Mr Martin steps out and hugs her. The accompanying villager turns out to be a young Israeli backpacker. Seeing her in safe hands, he makes a peace sign and slips away. Carlos watches from a distance, not knowing how to react. Lisa walks up to him and gives him a tight slap.

7

A Pool Emergency

Tara logs in at work on Monday morning in a foul mood. There were ten missed calls on her mobile late on Saturday night. Exhausted from cleaning fish tanks all day, she had slept early. Then Nalesh called on Sunday afternoon and gave her a blow-by-blow account of what transpired at the picnic.

Tara was aghast. Such a thing would never have happened if she was around!

According to the secretaries, Mr Martin has declared today an additional holiday *only* for the picnickers. Tara is upset that he's rewarding them for their carelessness. And so are the secretaries. Some of them feel a sense of comradeship with her, coming over to make small talk, trying to wheedle out information about the picnic. Tara's lips are sealed.

With the Carnaval a few days away, her workload is pretty light. Everyone is busy prepping and preening to give Martins' any work. After completing her lone assignment, she'll return to office and stay late, just in case there is some emergency. She knows there won't be any, but she's been asked to hold fort while the picknickers recuperate from their disastrous picnic.

There's always a lull at this time of the year, and not just at Martins', it's everywhere. The last few days before the Carnaval are notorious for dismal attendance at offices and learning institutions. A holiday mood prevails as people make plans to attend parties and dances held during those four days.

The Red & Black, The Red, Black & Gold, The Blue & White – all popular Carnaval dances in Goa are named after the colour scheme of their dress code. Artists apply finishing touches to tableaus and floats in makeshift workshops that mushroom overnight on street corners. Everyone gets ready to participate in the most important event on the Goan calendar – the Carnaval, and the Carnaval Float Parade. A four-day costume party; ninety-six hours of complete mad hatter fare!

After those four days of hyperactivity and madness, people slowly turn their attention to cleaning. Lakes and ponds that are choked with streamers and buntings. Barges and docks lined with garbage from boat parties. This is a crucial time for Martins' Dredging, their peak season. While Goa lies wasted on the floor, they wait eagerly for their telephones to ring. For the receptionist to mouth those hallowed words, "Hello, this is Martins' Dredging Pvt Ltd, how may I help you?"

Phone courtesy is not Tara's forte. Answering calls is the worst part of working late. Every other call is invariably a wrong number, a heavy breather or a frantic client whose job can easily wait till next morning. She barks a loud, "What?" into the receiver. "Yes, this is Martins' Dredging. What do you want?"

"Carlos Rodriguez please," says a male voice, speaking in a strange accent.

"Not here," Tara replies.

"Carlos does not work at Martins' Dredging?"

"He does, he's not in today."

"May I have his number?"

"Are you a friend, foe or relative of Carlos?" Tara asks.

"What? No! I have a pond that requires de-silting."

"Oh! It's work related. Call tomorrow morning after 10.30, okay?"

"Is he definitely coming to work tomorrow?" the caller asks.

"God knows! Call tomorrow and find out. Goodnight."

She's about to disconnect, when she hears the caller still speaking at the other end.

"Ma'am, let me finish… "

"Yes, please!" Tara says reluctantly.

"Can someone else do the de-silting?"

"Sure. But can it wait? I mean, if it's not an emergency. You see, the carnaval is coming… only two or three divers will show up tomorrow. After Carnaval, we'll have our full force. And by the way, it's the same at other firms," she quickly adds. "Nobody works at this time."

"But, that'll be a problem."

"That's just how it is… "

"Can those few who show up, do it? No problem if it takes longer. I'll pay three times the amount. The pond *has* to be de-silted before Carnaval," the caller emphasises.

"We need to survey your site, make estimates, get approvals, take an advance, hire equipment. Only then work starts. It takes time."

"I'll pay full advance, on the spot. Don't care how much it costs. Please, this is urgent," the caller's tone becomes increasingly restless.

"We can't ignore procedures because you're throwing money at us", Tara is miffed.

"Are you stalling me? Your visiting card says Martins' Dredging works 365 days a year, irrespective of public holidays."

"For emergencies and search and rescue ops."

"This *is* an emergency! If the pond is not de-silted, there'll be no party. It can't be cancelled, flyers are out."

Tara is exasperated. Another silly client with a pool party on his lawns. Martins' should stop listing swimming pool clean ups on their visiting card. But, it brings quick money with zero challenge.

"Sir, if forty people had drowned in that pool of yours and needed to be fished out, *that* qualifies as an emergency," Tara says, struggling to keep calm.

"A pond, not a pool! If I don't get it cleaned, more than forty people *will* die. Will you accept my work only then?" He thunders. "It's a massive freshwater pond, stagnant for decades… so dangerous."

Tara takes a deep breath and swallows her pride, "Sorry for misunderstanding. Message or email me your address, I'll be there tomorrow morning. Is 7 a.m. okay? I can come earlier."

"Just send the divers. You don't need to come."

"I *am* a diver."

Tara clears her table and prepares to leave. Conveniently, the juniors are never around when she needs them, especially Carlos. She vividly remembers his first day at work. How horrified she was when Mr Martin assigned him to her.

"Here's your toughest project, Tara. Make him a diver and I'll double your salary," he had said, coolly walking away, not bothering to find out if she wanted the raise. It turned out she did. Six years have passed and he's still a rookie. Likely he will remain one for the rest of his career, de-silting and cleaning ponds.

For all his awkward moves under water, Carlos moves really well above. The girls from his *vaddo*[8] patiently wait their turn during local fêtes. Ready to give an arm and a leg just to dance with him, so well he moves his tall, lithe frame. But Carlos only dances with her. Goddess Tara of two left feet! As she misses her cues and stomps his feet, amputees prop themselves on crutches around the dance floor and let out a collective sigh.

He visits her on most nights, to chit-chat and relish Aajji's food. Some nights after a disastrous date, he comes to vent his frustration. Falling asleep in her courtyard, an unfinished complaint perched precariously on his lip. "But, I'm a woman too!" she protests, shaking him awake. "Bai, you're different," he mumbles groggily, not realising it sounds like a tired cliché.

Some nights, after guzzling two bottles of feni, he pretends her courtyard is a ballroom and starts shadow waltzing. Moving flawlessly, his arms around a perfect, imaginary dancer. On those nights, Tara is overcome by a desperate desire to be that dancer.

But those who dance beautifully under water are no good above.

---

8. Hamlet, part of a village

8

Casa de Paraíso

Tara's scooter refuses to start. After much kicking, she concludes it's a good thing. Being unfamiliar with the site location, she might end up going in circles.

Last night's caller had messaged an address of some village near Arambol – that's roughly twenty-five to thirty kilometres from Saligao. She decides to take a pilot instead.

Does she own a jet? Nah, not yet!

Taxi drivers in Goa are called pilots. Handsome young studs – some of them at least – riding motorbike taxis that can negotiate the narrowest snaking village road, or a wide city avenue. They zip at breakneck speed, forcing people to hold on tight while being delivered to their destination.

It is a great mode of transport for those who do not have luggage; baggage is of course, optional. Many a city-bred, female tourists' heart has been utterly devastated after one such ride. The locals and Tara prefer the convenience and the low fares. And one more thing, she no longer raves about the yellow-top Premier Padminis of Bombay.

Tara walks to the taxi stand at Saligao *tinto*. The pilot at the head of the line is old enough to be her grandfather, and his bike is equally ancient. She fixes the fare and sits pillion. They head towards the Mae de Deus crossroad, going past its whitewashed spires towards Arpora, then the beach roads to Anjuna-Vagator, and finally towards Siolim. Twenty-five minutes and even half the journey isn't complete. Over the new bridge and into Chopdem, Arambol is half an hour's distance from here.

At Arambol, her pilot stops to ask for directions. Nobody knows the exact location. Last night's caller was frantic about some pool or pond party. Numerous sea-facing restaurants advertise several parties – 'Rocking Party, Goa's Biggest Paaaarty, Poolside Grind'.

After half an hour of reading signboards, posters and enquiring with waiters, they decide to try an uphill road. A rock with a painted fluorescent arrow catches her attention. Instinct tells her to follow. After a kilometre or so, the road gets too steep for the old pilot and his bike.

Tara gets off and starts walking, leaving him to kick-start his stalled bike. She notices a wooden signboard with a smaller fluorescent arrow. A few metres up, there is a huge boulder and the road ends abruptly. A dead end. Unless, someone actually wants to die.

Behind the boulder, a cliff drops sharply to the sea. As she is about to turn back, Tara notices a narrow walkway made of pebbles, tiles and seashells, cut into the side of the boulder. A flimsy iron fence is the only protection against a fall into the sea. She gingerly checks it out; it loops around the boulder to join a flatter, table land hill. In the distance, a large mansion peeps through trees. Tara retraces her steps to the pilot.

"It's up there," she tells him, pointing to the cliff.

"Bai, it doesn't look safe," he warns her. She pays his fare and clambers up the path once again.

Walking with measured steps around the boulder, she breaks into a run on the flat hill till she arrives at a majestic wrought iron gate. Pushing it open, she steps tentatively into a twisted paradise.

Stretching beyond is a vast estate. Casa de Paraíso stands in its centre, the morning sunlight accentuating its butterscotch exterior. It is a two-storied mansion with many rooms opening out into semicircular, balustrade balconies. Massive teakwood doors at the main entrance have a pair of gold plated lion knockers, their nose rings missing. Subject to a punishing silence by an electric doorbell, the lions have ruefully relinquished their authority to summon denizens of the Casa. An ornate Coat of Arms sits above the doorframe, advertising the economic stature of its original owners.

Surrounding the Casa is a tropical garden; fish tail palms, areca nut and coconut palms stand like sentinels. The lower level of vegetation consists of hardy cactus, hibiscus, bougainvillea and weeds.

As Tara walks on a cobbled garden path, stray patches of shrubbery catch her attention. *Hello? Is it? It is indeed Marijuana!* No wonder the name, Casa de Paraíso. It certainly is!

A little further, she notices an old fashioned greenhouse of glass and metal. Wiping a hole on a fogged windowpane, she peers inside. Her curiosity is amply rewarded. Mushrooms and hemp are growing in neatly arranged rows. *A hothouse of hallucinogens.*

What must she do to stay lost for a lifetime in a paraíso like this?

But before that, the pressing matter of a desilting has to be looked at. Veering back on course, she walks to the main door and rings the bell. Standing with her back to the door, eyes glued to the garden, she continues ringing, finger firmly on the switch, hoping someone will answer quickly. He lifts her offending finger and separates it from the switch. Startled she turns around, and comes face to face with him.

Standing before Tara is Bholenath Guruji. Not *a* Guruji or even *her* Guruji. Not anymore, at least. Her heart sinks as she realises her scooter was indeed trying to warn her this morning.

⚓

In 1961, Goa was liberated from its autocratic, slave-trading Portuguese rulers. After nearly four hundred and fifty years, the Portuguese were driven out by India. The liberators sucked Goa into the larger Republic. Many Goans followed their fleeing masters to Portugal and other European countries, while the less adventurous escaped to Bombay. They left behind large mansions and sprawling properties in the care of aged parents or grandparents. The ones who stayed behind did it out of love for the land. And some were just lazy perhaps.

Integration with India opened Goa's borders. Goans could now roam freely all over India, but it also meant that the rest of India could travel to Goa. This tiny paradise, dressed in pristine beaches and rolling hillsides, was no longer an island unto itself. Exposed to poverty, corruption and filth brought to their newly-opened doors, Goans could not help but wonder – had it all been worth it? 'The good old days, will they ever return?' became an oft-repeated lament.

Sitting in their *balcãos*[9] late into the night, they mulled over their bygone Goa. "Such a wonderful place this was when the Portuguese were around," they rued. "Just like a European country, so efficiently ruled. Look at us now, our once clean and orderly streets are covered with *paan-patti* spittle…"

Against this backdrop of angst and disenchantment, arrived the first wave of hippies, in 1968, seven years after Liberation. They received a red carpet welcome. Goans were extremely generous, opening their homes and their hearts to them. Of course, the hippies had no idea it was being done out of nostalgia for their white skin. For Goans, it wasn't the same as having the Portuguese back, but it was the next best thing. Goa must have appeared like the Promised Land for travel-weary hippies. The locals were friendly, fluent in Portuguese and English, and many dressed in western attire. Hindus coexisted peacefully with Catholics, making it a wonderful blend of the East and the West. Taking off their backpacks and guitars, the hippies settled down. Bholenath Guruji was one of them.

---

9. Sit out or balcony in a Goan house

Certainly, he wasn't Bholenath Guruji when he arrived in 1969. Probably a Tom, John, Harry or some other bland western name. A failed American musician who did not make it to the list of performers at Woodstock, he arrived in Goa to lick his wounds, hoping to reinvent himself and his music.

It's easy to imagine how the hippie music scene started in Goa. On a secluded beach during a full moon night, a few friends gathered with some smokes, drinks and guitars. Spreading beach mats around a bonfire and jamming. Wayfarers, musicians and listeners soon joined in as news spread through word of mouth. The sessions grew larger and louder. Experiments in music and dance were made in the same spirit as those with substances. Results of both either took off or crashed.

But no one complained; it was too early to tell if any damage was being done. With the crowds came the people who specialised in catering to them: chaiwallas, drug peddlers, trinket sellers and food shacks. A new way of being came into existence – the doped beach junkie at his dope music soiree. In other words, Rave parties!

The music evolved as the years passed. Simple acoustic sessions gave way to electronic ones. Till it arrived at a distinct sound that was christened 'Goa Trance' and played during full moon parties called Goa Trance Parties. Like ancient shamanistic rituals, these parties induced a trance-like state in the participants, altering their consciousness with a combination of psychotropic substances and frantic repetitive bass beats. Ultraviolet strobes heightened the effect further, pushing people off the edge.

In those early days, only hippies organised and attended these parties. Goans looked down on this raw, visceral music, their taste leaning towards Indian or Western classical. The dancing at these parties was like mass hysteria. Catholic Goans, adept at all forms of ballroom dancing, could not relate to it. Only the simple fisher folk and aboriginals, still in touch with their pagan traditions, understood.

Goa Trance evolves and mutates even today, unfettered and unmindful of protests by the local populace. Of course, the official government line is that these parties do not exist. They never did!

9

Bholenath Guruji

Bholenath Guruji greets her with a namaste. "You must be from Martins' Dredging. My sound engineer spoke to you last night."

"I'm Tara," she reciprocates with a namaste.

"I'm Bholenath. Come, let me show you the pond."

They walk around the mansion to where the pond is located. Soon she's trailing him by a few steps. She quickens her pace to match his, to walk by his side. He is faster than her.

Engrossed in his own thoughts, he

marches without taking his eyes off the ground. She prays for him to look at her. *Just for a second?* He gives her that same lopsided, crooked teeth grin, and is lost to her again. It makes her want to scream – "*It's me! Tara!*"

But why would he remember her name? Did she ever tell it to him?

She did, a few minutes ago…

Truth be told, Tara was just an insignificant entity amongst thousands who had squirmed and writhed at his parties in Goa, faceless people trying pathetically to register a blip on his radar. Bholenath Guruji was supremely unaware of his own charisma then, as he is now. Besides, he can hardly be expected to remember each and every person who attends his raves.

His dreadlocks have grown to waist level, the *rudraksh malas* around his neck have multiplied. Attired simply in a saffron kurta over maroon pyjamas, he looks shorter, pot-bellied, mellow and old. The wrong side of sixty.

Memories locked for years free themselves like a breached dam. This man used to haunt her dreams, occupying precious mind space even during waking hours. Bholenath Guruji held her in a mesmerising grip. Only, at that time it felt like a liberating embrace. A fifteen-year-old Tara was drawn to that embrace, to bask in its glow. Its radioactive aftermath, she is still suffering.

A Goan child growing up in Bombay, Tara was fed the mythology of Goa; a bedtime diet of ghost stories and hippie stories.

She particularly enjoyed the hippie stories. Her mother would enthral her with tales of young, impressionable, white men and women living in thatched huts rented from Goan fisher folk. They had chucked affluent lifestyles in the West for a frugal life in Goa. Little Tara was captivated by her mother's wacky descriptions of their skinny-dipping, their collective lunacy at Full Moon parties, and their bizarre music.

Determined to grow up fast and join them, Tara was convinced their life was more exciting than her own; or her parents' for that matter. She was afraid the hippies would disappear from Goa by the time she was old enough to leave Bombay and join them.

Tara heard the name Bholenath Guruji for the first time from her mother. He was among the early settlers in North Goa. According to her stories, this man was an enigma. A musician and a shaman, he was on a mission to save lost souls with his music. But very few people had actually seen him. He had no fixed address and no name. People called him whatever they wished – usually names reserved for gods and sages. Maybe he wasn't even real, a hologram. An image of the man, not the man himself!

So who was the real man? Where was he?

Every night Tara asked these questions, and every night her mother concocted newer, more fascinating answers. Bholenath Guruji did not exist in this world; he was from a different dimension parallel to ours. He lived on another continent and projected himself into Goa. According to some theories, he was either spirit matter or stardust.

Tired of imagining, Tara grew desperate to see him in person. Of course she did not voice her desire; it would have prompted a house arrest.

Fifteen years ago, Tara set out on her quest. She had just completed her SSC exams and three months of vacation loomed ahead. Some older friends from her apartment block had finished their degree exams. They were all driving to Goa to celebrate.

Tara hitched her agenda to their WagonR, packing ample supplies of bravado, little else. She was going to search for her divine, dreadlock-sporting Bholenath Guruji. Convinced that he was just waiting to be discovered by her as he sat meditating or playing music on some secluded Goan beach.

On arrival in Goa, she separated from her friends and headed straight to Baga. Stretched out before her were rows upon rows of half-naked hippies. All of them matched her mother's description. Her mother had forgotten to mention one important thing – the average hippie's deep-rooted distrust of capitalism and its nefarious by-products, mainly shampoos and tangle-free hair conditioners. To Tara's untrained eyes, they all appeared to be Bholenath; they all had dreads in their hair.

She abandoned her search and reluctantly went to Anjuna to join her friends. They were staying at a cheap hotel, doing the regular tourist thingy; shopping at flea markets and dancing in the hotel disco to Remo's Bombay Masala songs.

Going to Goa was *de rigueur* for Tara, as commonplace as boarding a slow Churchgate local from Andheri. All it took was a one-hour flight or an overnight bus journey. It meant staying at her ancestral home and visiting vast armies of relatives. Hour-long lunches and formal sit-down dinners, not this half naked loitering and feasting at funky cafés that she was indulging in on this trip with friends. Her parents would never have approved of such behaviour; it was the prerogative of tourists.

Being anonymous in Goa was therefore a dream come true for Tara. She quickly forgot about the mystical Bholenath Guruji. Perhaps he was a figment of her mother's warped imagination.

Tara didn't want to waste another minute thinking about how and where to find him.

One evening, after an exciting but tiring trip to Mackie's Saturday Night Market, Tara lay restless in bed, unable to sleep. It was unusually hot and still; even the palm fronds had stopped whispering. But insects were broadcasting their chatter over speakers, grating her nerves. And then, strains of an unfamiliar music wafted across, seeking her ears. Tara wondered if it was coming from the open-air beach disco. She parted her window curtains to check – there was nobody on the beach. Her friends were fast asleep so she left quietly to investigate, drawn to the music like a moth to a flame. After walking a kilometre on the cool sand, she stopped. Up ahead on a cliff, the sky was being criss-crossed by colourful moving lights. A blue aura floated above.

Just when she had given up hope of ever seeing one, Tara chanced upon her first trance party. She clambered up the hillock and landed smack in the middle of a crowd dancing without a care in the world. Awestruck by their frenzied movements, she stood on the periphery and watched. A boisterous bunch pulled her inside. Someone stuck a chillum in her mouth. Casually taking a drag she thanked him, her initiation complete.

On the stage stood Bholenath Guruji.

Tara recognised him at once, like a lost child recognises a parent in a sea of a million strangers. Their eyes met, and something clicked. An amalgamation of a dishevelled yogi and a crazed rock star, he was exactly what she had imagined.

The next day they returned home to Bombay. Tara's parents teased her about her sun tan and the money wasted on flea market trinkets, but failed to notice the irreversible chain reaction that had been set into motion inside her.

After that brief *darshan* of Bholenath Guruji, Tara was compulsively drawn to Goa, to get her fix of many more darshans. Always accompanied by the same set of friends, somehow these trips never coincided with her father's trips to Saligao. Thankfully, the party season in Goa is winter while the fruit-plucking season is summer.

'Going to Goa to meet Aajji and cousins,' became a repeatedly flogged excuse. Not once did her parents look askance, or ask pointed questions. And so it continued for many years. Departing early on Saturday mornings, Tara and her friends would reach Goa by nightfall. A quick shower and they were ready to party. And what parties they were!

The night advanced like sand through a sieve. Music seeped through skin into veins, travelling upwards to the brain. Circuit completed, their bodies charged with an unbelievable energy, lifting off to other dimensions. Entire lifetimes could be lived here, in the spaces between music loops.

This was Bholenath Guruji's realm. Initiator, Shaman, Masterful Manipulator of Beats Per Minute, he was Shiva reincarnated as a DJ – unleashing destruction and creation simultaneously on the crowd. Freeing people from their restrictive bodies and propelling them to outer space. Vibrating to divergent frequencies, they were released into the universe like so many unstable atoms.

After every performance, her friends returned to their hotels or shacks, but not Tara. She waited for Bholenath Guruji to step off the stage. This was the moment she had rehearsed a million times. Boldly stepping forward she would say, "I know you, Bholenath Guruji, even though you don't know me. You've talked to me in my dreams... I ..."

He would walk towards her, tousle her hair, and shove half-smoked joints into her palms, while she stood paralysed and tongue-tied.

The years passed and Tara blossomed into a confident young lady. She tasted academic success and it unlocked many more freedoms. The Goa Trance trips continued. She still hung around after every party, but now, she routinely helped with dismantling and packing the equipment. Trance parties in Goa are held furtively, so after one is over, the traces of it have to be cleared immediately. Help of any kind, especially if free, is much appreciated.

Tara slowly made friends with the technicians and crew members. Some nights she would carry Aajji's home-cooked meals in her backpack, which the technicians and Bholenath Guruji devoured hungrily. Soon, she was being invited to their inner circle after-parties, where potent drugs were consumed, unlike the garden variety peddled to the crowd. One night Tara saw her chance with Bholenath Guruji, and shamelessly seized it. The cocktail of drugs wore off the next day. In the cold light of early morning sobriety, she walked to Aajji's house, threw herself on the first available bed, and slept like a log.

Growing up, moving on, Tara has dived headlong into work. Her life revolves around Martins' Dredging, Mormugao Port and her aquariums of starfish. The partying of her teenage years is all but a faded memory.

How would she have known that her past was waiting to creep up on her? Today, of all days, a day involving routine work, de-silting and pond purification. At one time she had gone to seek Bholenath Guruji. But, it seems life has come full circle.

Gurur Brahma gurur Vishnu; Gurur devo Maheshwara
Gurur sakshat param Brahma; Tasmai shri Gurave namah

10

Balgo

The Casa lawn slopes gradually towards a cliff overlooking the sea. Arambol beach stretches below. In the distance, Mandrem and Morjim beaches are faintly visible amidst lush coconut groves. These three beaches are the last bastions of Goa's Hippy culture. The hippies have moved further from their '70s' haunts of Calangute and Baga, to seek quieter locales. They have made the most of what Goa has offered them – tolerance and a surrogate home.

They grow organic vegetables and fruits, run vegan salad bars, administer reiki and shiatsu massages, and enjoy their moonlit parties on beaches and in wooded forests.

Doing all this courtesy an unwritten code – they do not interfere with the locals, and the locals leave them alone. They stick to the beach belt mostly, rarely moving in the interiors and main cities.

Scattered paraphernalia around the lawn indicates a trance party is on the cards. Stepping over cables, amplifiers, speakers and lights, Tara and Guruji walk beyond the lawns. Halfway through, a young man joins them. Bholenath Guruji introduces

him, "My sound engineer, Balgo. He'll brief you. Bye, nice meeting you, Tara."

Tara smiles at Balgo. He had forgotten to divulge his name last night – not that she asked either. Stunned by the similarities in Balgo and Bholenath Guruji, Tara is amused by how much they appear like the quintessential *guru* and *chela*.

He walks with her towards a massive, gnarled banyan tree. A small Shiva temple nestles underneath its wide canopy. Few metres ahead is an ancient pond with stone steps leading down to its water. A bathing tank built on a natural underwater spring, it was used by devotees before praying at the temple.

Plastic bags, pet bottles and dried foliage floating on its surface make it look like an open garbage pit. Silt at the bottom has hardened to a rock like consistency, blocking the spring. Diverting it and causing it to break out in new openings. A few patches on the lawn are always sodden as a result.

The pond presents a unique problem. Decades of neglect have weakened its walls. Operating heavy drills in and around could cause an implosion, draining its murky contents into the lawn. The steps are in a state of utter disrepair, with edges worn off and blocks of stones missing. At most, they will withstand the vibrations of a water-pumping machine, rest of the cleaning will have to be done manually, Tara concludes.

Now to file a report, make an estimate, get costs approved, organise machinery and labour. It means a trip to Martins' and back to the Casa as quickly as possible. She hates the assignment already. If they weren't in such a hurry to have the party, she could have easily started the job tomorrow.

Balgo walks her to the back gate – which is the exit and entry to the Casa, not the precarious path she took to arrive. That path is the handiwork of a crazy sculptor who goes around Goa transforming rocks and boulders into works of art. Tara casually tells Balgo that she was a regular at Bholenath Guruji's parties in her teenage years. Elated, he promptly invites her for this one, saying it's super exclusive.

Tara returns at 3.30 p.m. with a generator, a pumping machine and hand-held wet drills. The hired migrant labourers had arrived before her and are now snoozing under a tree. Waking them up, she gets them started on the preliminary cleaning work, while she installs underwater and overhead floodlights. These will improve visibility and enable her to work at night. The pumping machine is fitted with an extra long outlet pipe, to drain the pond water into the sea below. As the pump begins flushing out sludge, the labourers start clearing surface garbage.

Tara's work will begin after a sufficient quantity of sludge is pumped out. Then she will manually scrape off solidified mud that is blocking the spring, using a wet drill where required and a pick axe. The entire de-silting will take fifteen hours, and only after that can the process of water purification start. Tara changes into her wetsuit, wears a full face helmet, straps on her oxygen tank and steps inside the pond.

Water is a great leveller. Flattering and streamlining bodies, regardless of shape and size, but not here and not today. Pregnant with filth, it has lost its clarity. Anyone else would feel trapped and weighed down, not Tara. She finds freedom in enclosed spaces, flitting effortlessly between the closed world below and the open vistas above.

The underwater and overhead lights do little to improve visibility; they barely penetrate the water surface. Swimming into this thick, dense liquid, she reaches the bottom and waits for the water level to drop to ten metres. Familiarising herself with the pond, she runs her hands lightly over its base, feeling for cracks and temperature variations caused by escaping air – which will tell her where the openings are. Unclogged, they will let the spring gush inside once again.

Toiling down below, Tara is envious of a different life being lived above. Where breathing comes effortlessly and is taken for granted. She checks her pressure gauge; there is enough air in her tanks. Little by little, she dislodges clumps of hardened silt. It is a drudgery to do this manually.

But thirty feet above, people indulge in the sensory pleasure of having sun tan lotions rubbed on to naked skin. Sweating profusely, Tara wonders *how long will it take for the pond to drain completely*? Her sweat reeks of rubber. Her body has turned into a self-cooking recipe; bones stir flesh, skin congeals, forming a layer on flesh – all sheathed inside a heat-preserving, body-protecting, Hazmat suit.

The water pump's outlet pipe disconnects and falls inside the pond. Surfacing with it to reprimand the labourer whose lookout it is, Tara sees a sight that makes her blood boil. The labourers are moonlighting on her time. Rubbing sun tan lotion onto four nubile nymphets, they have switched camps.

Storming outside the pond, she marches towards the four men and admonishes them. A heated exchange ensues, peppered with choicest Hindi swear words – Tara throwing in a few Marathi and Konkani ones for good measure. The labourers trot off in a huff, aluminium tiffin carriers clanking angrily with each step. They have already earned three times what she will pay them, by way of *baksheesh* from the sunbathing guests.

Tara is in a fix. Organising new labour at such a short notice is impossible in Goa, and besides, they too will be distracted by the sideshow on the lawns. She is overcome by a sudden urge to chase away the sunbathers. Like her grand aunt from Calangute was infamous for doing in the seventies. The old lady in a *kashti* would patrol the beach in front of her house with a cane. She'd wait till the hippies had stripped, applied suntan lotions, and pulled out their favourite books or chillums. Then, she would spring into action. *Whack, whack, whack*, she'd chase them all over the beach, leaving angry welts on their fair naked backs.

But only one-fourth of the task is complete. Doing it by herself will take thirty hours. The assignment's degree of difficulty has doubled all of a sudden. Angry and frustrated, she remembers Gregory's words, *hands crisscrossed with cuts.*

Working feverishly through the afternoon, she pumps out a large quantity of sludge. By late evening, a deliciously dull ache radiates through her every muscle and sinew. Like a rubber band entwined between fingers of two palms, her body feels stretched simultaneously in different directions. It will snap if she continues.

Tara calls it a night at 3.30 a.m. Before switching off the overhead and underwater lights, she observes her work from a terrestrial perspective provided by the highest pond step.

The pond looks inviting, glowing like the rectangular dial of a nightglow watch. The natural spring, trickling in weakly, is being supplemented by tanker water. It no longer smells of rotting garbage and even though the water is a mossy shade of green, she reckons it will do for a swim. Peeling off her diving suit, Tara steps inside. The cold water is a shock to her system. Corseted all day inside a rubber suit, limbs covered with gloves and flippers, her body is at a higher temperature. Liquid radium cools it down.

"Been dying to do that for so long…"

Tara turns to check who it is, not expecting anyone to be awake at this hour.

"… but the water was so vile. *Look* at it now!"

She smiles, "Still some work left."

"If you can swim in it, so can I!"

Stripping right in front of her, Balgo dives in. She tries not to concentrate on his nakedness, or hers. It *is* difficult. After all, it's not like she regularly skinny-dips with clients, nor is it listed under 'occupational hazards' in the Martins' divers' handbook.

"So Tara, you specialise in cleaning ponds?"

"Hope not," she laughs. "I'm trained in Offshore and Inshore diving, Hazmat diving and Search & Rescue. Actually, I specialise in precision welding on ships and cables. On a bad day I clean ponds, swimming pools, fish tanks…"

"Apologies for giving you a bad day…"

"No problem, cleaning ponds is better than being a telephone operator, no?"

Balgo smiles sheepishly and starts drumming on the water surface, sending shimmering ripples in her direction. The underwater lights appear incandescent, blurring the contours of their bodies. She looks up; it's her turn to make polite conversation.

"So Balgo, I heard you're taking over from Bholenath Guruji. Is he retiring after this party?"

"No way! Why is everyone spreading stories! I'm just taking care of minor details." He looks around, making sure they don't have an audience. "Apart from sound management, which I always do, Guruji has delegated decoration to me this time.

"I asked about using the pond and he said, 'You have the money, if we can afford the clean-up without compromising on lights and sound, go ahead.' The pond's going to look fantastic, thanks to you, Tara."

"Can't say it's been a pleasure, but a job's a job."

"The party will make up for this, I promise. There'll be floating lights on water, and I've ordered lotuses. Lights and lotuses, just like the old days… People will skinny dip, like us," he says, reminding her once again that they are naked.

It's almost dawn. She wants to catch an hour's sleep before starting the next day's toil. Her wetsuit is on the topmost step. Had it been on her, she would have heaved herself out and bid him goodnight. Sans wetsuit or swimsuit, it will make for an inelegant sight.

"I have to sleep, you know…" she tells him.

"Oh, of course…"

Stepping out, he provides her a sumptuous view of his butt. A strange looking serpent is tattooed at the base of his spine. Tara has seen all kinds of tattoos on all kinds of bodies, but none like this one. He picks his clothes from the steps, but does not wear them. Looking over his shoulders he says goodbye, climbs the steps and disappears into the pitch darkness beyond the floodlights.

11

Casa de Trance

The stage is up and ready, the sound systems are in place, and yet it looks as if something is amiss. She recognises at once the glaring absence of a backdrop. What's a trance party without a backdrop?

Freaky, wacky and psychedelic, a stage backdrop acts like a nucleus to focus one's energy. Works of art created on wings of ecstasy, they are the feverish renderings of stoned artists.

The artist commissioned for the backdrop is deep in the throes of his most amazing trip, immersed in visions that are yet to be transferred on a canvas sheet. Balgo is outraged; he has to be physically restrained from visiting the artist. *Let him slash his wrists on the canvas. Even that will do for now.*

A young technician capitalises on the opportunity, fashioning an impromptu backdrop with a tie and dye silk sari. In its centre, he spray paints a Nataraja. Then, in a wonderful fusion of painting skills and electrical wizardry, he highlights it with blinking fairy lights to create the illusion of movement. The Nataraja actually dances!

Below the cliff, the sun has bid goodbye, painting the sky in shades of vermilion. As twilight falls, the evening breeze bristles with electricity. Trees strung with colourful lights come alive. UVs, strobes, fluoros, lasers and smoke machines are switched on for a rehearsal, setting the sky ablaze with holograms and fantastic light patterns.

Tara is still wearing her wetsuit. Seven or eight hours have passed since her tasks were completed. Oddly, no one finds it unusual, a fully kitted diver casually strolling in their midst. Should she bother changing at all? Nobody will notice for sure. All the party people will arrive doped, and the presently sober organisers will quickly get down to the business of getting high.

But she does not fancy being cooked inside her own dive suit. The heat generated by dancing and smoking at a trance party can make the flimsiest of clothing feel like steel-plated armour. She has packed a red halter-top with gold sequins, and denim shorts for the party. She rushes to her tent for a quick shower and change. As she is about to enter, she hears grunting coming from inside. Peeking tentatively, she spies a young couple on her bed. Tara contemplates being the only one dressed for a costume party. Maybe lug cylinders to complete the look!

But the heat is bothering her, and it's not just the energetic lovers who are responsible. She tiptoes inside, finishes her tasks quietly and tiptoes out. They seem so oblivious to the world though, even an earthquake would fail to disengage them.

The gardens of Casa de Paraíso start filling up with groups of people standing in tight circles. Leaning against a lit up tree, Tara watches the crowds. The lights reflect off her sequinned top making her shimmer like a Christmas decoration. A veteran of many trance parties, she can't believe it is her first time solo. She has no agenda. Of course, there's dancing to be done, and drugs, but how much, and for how long? Simple decisions weigh heavily when one is alone. Just then she sees Balgo walking towards her.

"All set?" she asks, rather enthusiastically.

"No! Damn, work just doesn't end. I turn a corner and see something I've forgotten," Balgo responds.

"Balgo! It's time."

"Shit, it is! Okay Tara, I'm at the sound controls if you need me. Oh, I almost forgot why I came here," he says and moves closer to hug her. "Welcome back!"

At fifteen, Tara took her first step into the Goa trance scene. She felt welcomed like never before. Everything was unusual, the music, the people, even clothing. Clothes that looked plain by day came alive by night under UV lights; revealing secret patterns and messages. She discovered how easy it was to change her mood by popping pills, and expand her mind by inhaling substances. Like living in a greenhouse, where a sense of well-being could be summoned at will – albeit an artificial one, engineered and controlled with measured dosages.

Suddenly the real world paled in comparison. She became a pro at balancing the real world and the Goa trance world, never letting them overlap, never allowing one to know the other. And then, after five years of being a regular, one trance night, she screwed up. Or rather, got screwed. If only she had been less awestruck by the whole experience.

Ten summers have passed since that escapade. Ten summers that changed Tara's priorities and expectations from life. Now, as a professional diver, she experiences bigger highs by diving deeper and staying there longer. She is mastering the art of stretching compressed air to its limit. Flirting with death, she has realised, is a far superior trip.

So what is she doing at the Casa de Paraíso tonight? Why can't she be indifferent to the goings on, complete her work and bid goodbye?

She has meticulously avoided this scene for ten years; it is a constant reminder of the pain she inflicted on her family – her father in particular. So she blocked it out, and life has been smoother. There was no reason to even think about it.

But, a door opened. Tara walked in and landed smack in the middle of events and people from her past. A déjà vu, and yet, not quite!

Older now, with the maturity to see things differently, she hopes to undo some of her earlier damage. A face-off with her demons is on the cards. And then, hopefully, she will lay her mother down. Tara is still lugging her around; a lone pallbearer reeling under dead weight.

Bholenath Guruji climbs onstage through a haze of sandalwood incense. Bathed in UV, he looks unreal. He takes the microphone, signalling the crowd to be quiet, and thunders… "Tara! Tara Salgaonkar, come on stage."

She freezes, turning once again into her teenage self. Balgo whispers something to Bholenath Guruji, jumps off stage and starts walking in her direction.

"But-but, why does he want me up there?"

"Find out for yourself," Balgo says, guiding her through the crowd.

Bholenath Guruji gives Tara a hand, pulls her up on stage and hugs her. She looks into his grey green eyes with her own misty grey green ones, for some flicker of recognition, some acknowledgement of their shared past. There is none. He is genuinely happy to meet her in the present moment.

He bellows into the microphone, "Few days ago, Tara rang my doorbell so hard, it made me deaf. Who would've thought her fingers could also create magic?" He hugs her again. "She has single-handedly revived our old pond by the Shiva temple. Remember how filthy it was? Look at it now, it's filled with nectar!"

"And that chap over there," he points at Balgo, gesturing him to come up front. "This party is his baby, but he won't admit it."

Bholenath Guruji hugs Balgo. They look like a pair of jousting lions, their matted manes highlighted by blue UV. Tara thanks them both and leaves the stage. As she navigates the crowd, strangers smile at her and touch her. As if Bholenath Guruji's hug has led to transference of his energy. Every touch makes her squirm. The last thing she needs now is for her Dad to see all this on TV. But she need not worry. No local TV channels or even the national ones are covering this party. The camera crews present are mostly independent international ones; typical of all genuine Goa trance parties.

Bholenath Guruji starts his pre-party ritual. Tara is relieved to note it hasn't changed – the same *pooja thali*, the same brass Nataraja murti and pooja bell. Chanting a quick prayer to the lord of dance and music, he prostrates first to Nataraja, and then to his audience. And the mayhem begins!

The sky bursts into a thousand swirling holograms, as projectors shoot guided light missiles. UV lights dance over people, the sound wattage quickly escalates from double-digits to five digits. The party becomes a giant heart throbbing inside a body that is Goa.

On the other side of the mansion, the pond is filling to capacity. Floating lights and lotuses share space with human heads, all bobbing simultaneously. Tara looks at the pond and feels the satisfaction of a job well done. She walks along the periphery, marvelling at reflections on water. The hanging roots of the temple banyan tree are draped with strings of lights, like stars descending on earth. A few revellers use the roots to swing themselves over the pond and jump in.

Strolling back to the dance area, she reaches into her little pouch. Chillums, bongs and joints are being passed from person to person, shared in a spirit of brotherhood and bonhomie. Suddenly, a fistful of mushrooms are thrust into her palms, her unlit joints taken and passed on to the next person, who in turn passes them to another. Tara is distraught at the hijacking. But there's little she can do other than wait for the next round to begin, and hope someone else's joints land in her hands. Having tried mushrooms before, she knows they are wasted on her. But it will be impolite to discard them.

The music turns ballistic, progressing swiftly to industrial strength Psy-Trance. The crowd hoots its appreciation. Beats enter her ears and spill out a throbbing woofer in her forehead. Tara moves languorously, her earlier inhibitions gone. One by one, guest DJs take over, the music changing with every transition.

She barely notices – she's paying attention to something else. Her tongue feels like emery paper, maybe even looks like one, and there's a horrible metallic taste in her mouth.

Meanwhile Balgo takes a break and strolls through the crowds, stopping every now and then to greet someone. He spots Tara in the dance area; she is the lone statue. Coming over, he whispers, "Wow! Tara!"

She latches on to him and whispers back, "I can't feel my feet. I think it's a DCS attack! And I'm not even diving!"

Balgo bursts out laughing, "Compensating for ten years in one night? Pace yourself Tara!"

"Those crappy shrooms! Tasted worse than shit," she replies, sticking her tongue out and shuddering.

"Should've warned you, Tara. They aren't for amateurs."

"I'm a veteran! I've attended more parties than you."

He doesn't argue. "Okay, here's what will happen," he says, putting an arm around her shoulder. "After the numbness passes, you'll bounce in zero gravity, just the feeling," he clarifies, seeing her look of disbelief.

"Sit in a comfortable place – oh wait! Float on water! Yes! You've got to try it, Tara!"

"You try it," she snaps, "I can't move my feet." Suddenly she bursts into peals of laughter. "I'm a fish! Look pa, no feet!"

He helps her to the pond. Of course she can walk; her mind is playing tricks. It is playing up her fears actually. Once again, she is startled by the pond's beauty. It is getting prettier as the night progresses, or is it yet another illusion?

Moonlight plays hopscotch over the pond surface, dappling it in a silvery glow. On the steps, artists are busy painting faces and bodies of people. Turning them into psychedelic tribesmen dressed in fluorescent war paint. Tara walks past the coloured bodies and dives in – clothes and all. She swims to a quiet corner; the floating lights have drifted away, leaving it unlit and therefore deserted. A large crowd is gathered above the steps.

Standing in a circle, they watch a dancer doing a lurid dance. All heads in the pond are also turned in that direction. Exhibitionistic dancing is rare at trance parties, people dance in a uniform fashion to the repetitive beats. Tara wonders who the oddity is. Swimming closer, she sees a slight, perfectly shaped pretty thing, dressed in black leather pants and a magenta satin shirt. A bit difficult to comprehend whether it is a man or a woman. A teenaged Shiva in his avatar of Ardhanarishwara has come to bless Bholenath Guruji's party. Or not!

The transgender urges people to join him. Like a wind-up toy gone haywire, he dances frantically. Annoying people who aren't interested in his overtures. But he's no discriminator, this Ardhanarishwara; everyone gets felt up and felt against equally. Tara waits anxiously for the next set of events to unfold.

A trio of hefty guys surround the dancer and start feeling him up – not for pleasure, for a body search. Unsuccessful at retrieving what they're looking for, they start hitting him. They bash his face, split his lips and turn his beautiful round eyes into tiny slits. They lift him and fling him into the pond. He lies limp on the surface for a split second, then water closes in. People watch nonchalantly; as if chucking a dazed, battered person into a pond is the most normal thing.

Tara is stunned as onlookers and perpetrators disperse. Looking down at her own body, she checks if she's still in her Martin's wetsuit. She's not. Yet they expect *her* to do the job!

But it's an easy night. Saving supreme Ardhanarishwaras should be a breeze too. Tara tumble-turns and swims in his direction. Due to her earlier toiling, the clear water quickly reveals his fast sinking body. Lunging at him, she holds him by the waist, her leg wrapped tight around his lower body and starts to surface. Lifeless in her arms, head flopped on her shoulder, he lets himself be rescued.

All of a sudden he stirs, and looks into her eyes. It's difficult to say who is more startled. Tara, so used to retrieving dead bodies that she forgot this one is alive. Shocked as if he's seen a ghost, he struggles out of her grip. But then, he remembers that he can't swim. He comes back into her arms, and faints.

Tara is amazed by the lightness of his form, his slight but perfect musculature. Moments ago he was alive to the world, performing a wild passionate dance. Even his shoulder-length wavy hair had joined in. Slicked down and rendered limp by water, it now frames his badly disfigured face. She lays him on the steps and waits. He is breathing, but in a state of shock. From the corner of her eye she sees the trio marching towards her.

"He's a pickpocket," says the leader to Tara.

"So? Must you kill him?" Tara asks him.

"He stole our passports and wallets."

Tara is not convinced. "Do you have proof?" she asks him.

"That's why we threw him in the water. To make him talk."

"Dead people don't talk," she replies angrily.

"We would've saved him. But miss smarty pants thought it was a *Baywatch* audition and jumped in first."

Tara is so livid that she wants to throw her cylinder at them, but it's in the tent. Someone squeezes her shoulder. "You know him, Tara?" Balgo enquires, pointing at the manhandled mess, now conscious and sitting upright on the steps.

"She knows me," says the accused, looking at Tara with what would've been pleading eyes, had they not swollen into slits.

"I know him," Tara plays along.

"Can you vouch for his character?" asks a wizened hippie.

"Sure. I, Tara Salgaonkar, solemnly declare this person all of you have mercilessly beaten, is *not* a pick-pocket."

Balgo apologises on everyone's behalf. The onlookers leave, and as with everything Tara rescues, she is left holding it. For a change it's a live body. But he can barely move. She carries him to her tent, puts him gently on her bed and looks for spare clothes that will fit him.

"Bai, I must leave, they'll kill me!" he says, suddenly sitting up, shaking like a leaf.

Tara runs to his side. "It's okay, you're safe now."

"Thought I was going to die today…"

"Where's the loot? Your stash, the stuff you stole… where have you hidden it?" she asks, exasperated.

"I'm not a thief, you only said so," he squeaks in his yet to break teenage voice.

"I said it to save your ass. C'mon, tell me!"

"Fine, here it is," he says, taking Tara's hand and pressing it on his crotch.

Blushing at the feel of his hard-on, Tara pushes him away. Before she can comprehend what just happened, a wad of notes and passports rolled tight, pops out of his leather pants.

He looks up at Tara and smiles. "Thank you for saving me, bai. Keep the cash, I'll take the passports. They'll get me good money in the black market."

12

Tara's Secret

Tara has the pond to herself after the incident. She swims lazy laps, synchronizing her strokes to music. Seeing her, some people dive in and start swimming in her path. Irritated, she tumble-turns and swims to the bottom. Sitting there, she views the party through a translucent wall of water.

Everyone seems to be dancing in slow motion. Thumping music sounds soothing and mellow, mirroring her own heartbeats. Breathing effortlessly, she feels no need to surface; her lungs have morphed into oxygen cylinders. As dawn streaks the skies above, Tara descends deeper into the spring, seeking the source of her existence.

The party runs out of steam at 7.30 a.m. Ambushed by a night of dancing and doping, people are asleep on the steps of the pond. Those precariously close to the water's edge have to be roused and sent to safer places. Some are leaving to catch the next flight or train. Tara enters her tent and finds strangers asleep on her bed, on the floor – every inch occupied. Wearily trudging to the Casa, she finds an empty room, takes off her soggy clothes and flops on a lumpy bed.

At mid-afternoon she wakes up, drenched in sweat. She wonders what it must be like in her outdoor tent, and is grateful to have found this room. At least it has an-old fashioned overhead fan. Sunlight filters through the tiny holes of a lace curtain above her bed. Pinholes of molten light inch closer with each passing minute.

Moving her bare body to avoid the advancing light, she bumps into something harder than a pillow.

It stirs. She feigns sleep. Balgo gets up quietly, not wanting to disturb her. She sits up. He acts surprised and says, "Oh, it's you. Didn't realise this bed was taken. Fifty freaks have crashed in my room, so I came here."

"Same situation in my tent. I'm leaving, you stay," Tara responds.

"Leaving now? So hot outside! I'm going to Assagao later, to return the equipment. Come with me Tara, catch a bus or a pilot to Saligao from there."

A few minutes later, she walks to the pond. Balgo joins her with two cups of steaming coffee. They sit in silence on the steps, watching the complete disarray of lotuses, beer bottles and burnt silver foil. Last night's ethereal pond is now filthy and real.

"Tara, how do I prevent garbage from collecting in the pond?"

"Simple! Cover it with tarpaulin. There's a shop at Mapuça Market. Give them material, they'll stitch."

"Will you come with me, please?"

"I'll ask Carlos to assist you… the guy you called up for, remember?."

"Glad I got *you*, Tara," he says. "Hope you enjoyed last night. I mean, what with the fight and all. Not the comeback party you expected, right?"

"Frankly Balgo, I had no expectations. A lot has changed."

"What's changed?"

"So many things, the trance scene was different in early millennium. Pure, more upbeat. Now everything is *jhataak*. Flashier lights, bloody powerful strobes – planes will fall out of the sky!" Tara says to Balgo.

"Evolution, Tara! You missed ten years. *You* did not keep up with the evolution in Trance. Take a crash course now. Attend every party with me this season."

"You kidding me? I'm so wasted! Thank goodness there's no work for next three days."

"I simply cannot imagine missing even one season. Were you locked up in Siberia for ten years?"

"Bet they have Goa Trance parties there too!" She smiles. "Actually, I was right here. We moved from Bombay to our ancestral home in Saligao when I turned twenty-two."

"Are you joking, Tara? You did weekend commutes from Bombay every party season. But when you moved here, you stopped attending? They were in your backyard, for god's sake!

"Precisely why."

"Meaning? *Oooh* is that how you play, Tara? Love the chase, but when it becomes accessible…"

"Not at all. I lost touch with friends after graduation. I did the party scene with them only. And I started working. You saw what my work involves, right?"

"Excuses, excuses!"

"Mom died… my partying killed her," she mumbles.

"Come again?"

"My partying killed my mother," Tara repeats, louder this time.

"She didn't approve?"

"She didn't *know*."

"Now that's a story. What happened?"

"I don't know. I mean I do, but still don't know why she did it."

"Suicide?" he asks her.

"Ya, I pushed her to commit suicide with my partying. Mostly that last party."

"What happened at this party?"

"Too many things, before and after. I got pregnant, had an abortion, returned from the clinic to a dead mother. Can you believe it! I killed two generations with one abortion!" Tara starts laughing. Balgo is not amused.

"Mom left a note saying she failed me. Actually, I failed her. I failed myself. So I swore – 'No more trance parties'. End of story."

"So... why are you here?"

She stares at her feet intently. She takes a deep breath and sighs. "I think I... I'm a sucker for punishment. Thought I could undo some of my mistakes, or *at least* forgive myself for making them."

"Have you, Tara?"

"No. Not easy."

"Tara, your mother's death was destined. She would've died *even* if you had missed that party – maybe differently, but nevertheless. It's karma."

Tara stands up, she is agitated. "Karma *sharma* is just bullshit that we Indians package and sell to you westerners. Don't you dare sell it back to me."

Balgo tugs at her hand and makes her sit down. "Sorry. I am truly sorry, Tara. I didn't mean to be patronising. Please, just sit and talk," he says. "Or don't talk. But stop blaming yourself."

"Not possible," she says, tears streaming down her face.

The evening breeze gently pushes water against the embankment, creating a symphony with empty beer bottles. Selfishly engrossed in her own despair, Tara is oblivious to this music. She pays attention now. Closing her eyes, she imagines a different kind of party. Dressed in formal attire, the parents of last night's ravers are clinking glasses of champagne. A *Clube*

Nacional kind of 'Dine and Dance' extravaganza. The jazz band plays *Nica's Dream*.

The composition strikes a false note, subtle yet recognizable to her expert ears. As lotus leaves quiver, her hair stand on end; it is a sound she is all too familiar with. Water displaces slightly, signalling a surreptitious movement underneath. She holds her breath. A few metres ahead, between clumps of lotus leaves, a face appears above water.

Tara watches as the rest of the body surfaces. A young woman's naked body. Alabaster white and delicately chiselled, like a life-size Lladro figurine. The setting sun anoints her with streaks of gold. A halo of orange hair around her head has strips of silver foil entangled here and there, like she ran out of a celestial salon in the midst of a hair colouring. Feet together, hands by her side, there is firmness in her pose, but no rigidity.

Balgo squeezes Tara's hand searching for an explanation. She smiles, aware of the significance of this moment; it is his first time. His first glimpse of a drowned corpse. The nausea passes if you concentrate on its beauty, she wants to tell him, but cannot find words to string a sentence. She strokes his hand instead. They sit and wait, grateful that speech has deserted them, for speech impedes vision. Their reverence is rewarded with another offering, a naked young man. He surfaces parallel to the woman, facing the opposite direction. Michelangelo could not have sculpted a better David. And Adonis would have been so envious. Like a Norse god, he is tall and statuesque. Blond facial hair merges with a skin that's growing paler as they watch. He lies amidst lotuses, bottles and beer cans, a six-pack on his taut abdomen. Not breathing. Dead.

Dumbstruck by the stunning symmetry of death, they ponder over the precision with which both bodies surfaced. They hold on to this precious moment; it is all they can do. Police formalities will follow later, as things less sublime often do. For now, this is theirs to behold.

13

Gregory is Wait-listed

Gregory had met Tara at Martins' before leaving for Cochin; it was a work-related visit. She was dreadfully formal, as if nothing had happened between them. He assumed she didn't want her colleagues to know, and mirrored her behaviour.

Normally he looks forward to a Cochin assignment. He is emotionally attached to this quaint port town, having trained for two years at the INS Venduruthy, on Willingdon Island. Cochin took him – a shy boy from Goa, and moulded him into a confident young man. And a diver, of course!

He opted for a Cochin posting for the first five years of his naval career – the opportunities were better than Goa. But he had to return home due to family commitments.

Gregory envies Tara for the opportunities she's had in Bombay, to swim and to study. Google her name and thirty pages of search results show up with her swimming competition records, stats and pictures, followed by half a page dedicated to her work exploits at Martins'. As much as he admires her professionalism, her earnestness to complete the job at hand, today – not *phalyaan*[10], he sometimes wonders if it is Goa that is

10. Tomorrow (Konkani)

stopping Tara, or is it Tara. He can be forgiven for hanging around in Goa – he has old parents, vast ancestral property, and he's the only son. But there aren't any such compulsions for a Goan girl – especially one who has decided *not* to be domesticated. She should pay attention to her career if she doesn't plan to get married. Or does she.

The past three weeks he's been irritable and distracted at work. His superiors have ignored it, probably dismissing it as Carnaval fever. Goans contract it at this time of the year, getting cured only after those four days have passed. He suspects they're waiting for an opportune moment to pull him up. The sooner they do it, the better. It will force him to snap out of his stupid daydreaming.

To add to his woes, there are ten sari shops in the city with her name. Tara Saris, Tara Silk Emporium, Tara Handlooms & Cottons, Taarika Fashions. Seems like her name is a favourite here. Avoiding them is next to impossible – three are on his way to work. Tara, who has little use for saris, will be amused. "Wear a sari? Not even for my own wedding," he's heard her say. He wonders why she dislikes this beautiful garment.

Too much trouble, all those pleats. Total disaster when they come loose in the middle of a street.

So does she prefer a white gown with mother of pearl trimmings?

Enough of thinking, it's time for action. He wrangles a weeks' leave to go home for the Carnaval. Every year he has seen Tara at the dances with Carlos or some other diver colleague. This year *he* will ask her out.

Tara is a different person in civvies. And more so in party clothes – on those rare occasions when she wears them. All divers face a peculiar problem. As their faces are covered by breathing apparatus and goggles, their bodies in identical wetsuits, the only way to recognise them is by height and shape. The curve of someone's buttocks, the protrusion of someone's belly, becomes their calling card, resulting in comical scenarios when they accidentally bump into each other at the *tinto* or the *tiatr*, wearing regular, loose fitting civilian clothes. They apologise and carry on, not recognising each other.

Tara's problem is similar and yet different. Recognising her in a wetsuit is easy – she's the shortest at Martins' – not to mention, the only one with breasts. But the minute she steps out of her wetsuit, into the loose-fitting contours of a tracksuit, or baggy jeans and t-shirt, she becomes *any woman*. Many a times Gregory's colleagues have gone to Martins' and asked her to her face if Tara was in office. At the Carnaval, or during New Year's, someone will invariably point to Carlos and ask, "Who's that chick with him?" Go closer to investigate and remark dejectedly, "It's Tara."

Gregory is certain she will accept his invitation to the Red & Black Ball. He knows she likes him, even though she's standoffish towards him in public. He's figured one thing about her, behind that care-a-damn-attitude is a shy woman. Or a shy woman nursing old wounds; picking at the scabs every now and then, refusing to let them heal. He wonders why.

What she really needs is someone strong and stable. Like him. Yes, definitely. Him

And there'll be no woman superior.

It is *Sabado Gordo*[11], first day of the Carnaval, famous for the Carnaval Float Parade. Gregory feels the same excitement he did as a child when his dad would take him all the way to Panjim to watch the parade. This year, uncle Benny Da Costa has put up a float to promote his restaurant, Vista do Cais. The float, called *Ocean Fantasy*, is Gregory's design and concept and that is why he is eager for Tara to see it. But her mobile is switched off since morning, from the time he arrived from Cochin.

At 1.30 in the afternoon, she finally takes his call. "Benny has a float at the parade," he tells her excitedly.

"Who?"

"Oi! My chef uncle, forgot what?"

"Oh, okay, that funny chap… I'll see on TV."

"I've come all the way from Cochin, Tara. Don't do this."

"To see me?" Tara asks, sounding surprised.

"Yes! And the Carnaval parade."

"Forget the parade, come see me. I just completed a tiring assignment; it's my time-off."

"Okay, at least come for Red & Black with me."

"I'm going with Carlos. Already said yes to him."

"But you go with him every year, Tara!"

"Arrey, does it matter who I go with? I'll be there no, we can dance together. By the way, I suck at ballroom dancing, wear steel boots."

---

11. Fat Saturday *(Portuguese)*

Gregory gets on his bike and rides to Saligao. Her house looks so normal during daytime. Maybe she invited him at night just to spook him. But he's not running away this time. He rings her doorbell. After nearly five minutes, Tara opens the door.

"Aajji I don't feel like eating…" her eyes are closed like a sleepwalker.

"Hi Tara."

She opens her eyes, tries to focus, and then, "What the fff – gimme a break Gregory! Told you I don't want to see the parade."

"Tara, you okay?"

"For what you've come?"

"You only said, come see me. I was missing you Tara. "

"Some work or wot?"

"C'mon, you know what I mean." He blushes.

Tara is amused, she walks away, leaving him standing at the door. He shuts the door behind him and follows.

"I'm just tired ya. I snap at people when I'm like this. Better to lock myself, keep everyone out of harm's way, no?"

"Oi, why so tired? What assignment did you do?"

"I'm not telling. You'll start lecturing."

He's alarmed. "You got the bends? Again?"

"No! Just a stupid de-silting *re*. Look what's happened," she says, showing her painfully raw palms. "I remembered what you said at Vista do Cais… hands criss-crossed, something-something-something…"

He wants to kiss her palms and make them better. Instead, he bursts out laughing. "That's still stuck in your head! Good! You are thinking about what I said."

"I'm not leaving Martins'."

"Who said anything about that? C'mon, get ready in five minutes. We can still make it for the parade."

"Stop badgering me."

"I'll make some coffee for us. Get ready."

"Ai Saiba! I'll fall asleep standing, so tired I am."

"I've got VIP seats in the Chief Minister's enclosure. Sleep on those sofas. When something good comes, I'll wake you, okay?"

"Don't be ridiculous, Gregory. Nothing good will come. Floats get worse every year. I'll sleep at home only, thank you!"

"Something good *is* going to come. Ocean Fantasy! You *have* to see it!"

"Don't want to see any fantasy-shantasy. They're all the same: one big fish, one giant lobster, random sea shells, some sad looking coconut palms, and nylon nets! Lots and lots of nylon nets. They give them free at Mapuça market during Carnaval, I think."

"It's nothing like that, okay? I designed it. It's not like that at all, Tara!"

"Navy doesn't pay you? You're freelancing as a float designer? Tctchtch."

"I make enough, okay?"

"Then too much free time you have?"

"Oi! What more should I do? Fall at your feet?"

"Stop it, stop!" she starts laughing and jumping around, as he makes a big show of prostrating at her feet. "Okay, I'll come."

14

Panjim Float Parade

Float parades are the most spectacular part of the Goan Carnaval, organised in four main cities – Panjim, Margao, Vasco and Mapuça. The most important one, flagged by the state's Chief Minister, is the Panjim City Float Parade. It opens the Carnaval, a four-day pagan celebration brought by the Portuguese when they stepped on Goan shores.

Just a few days before Carnaval, the identity of the man chosen to play King Momo is revealed at a press conference organised by Goa Tourism. King Momo is a make believe monarch. The only qualification required to apply for his 4-day job is a big paunch. He leads the parade in a spectacular float, surrounded by a bevy of beauties. Declaring Goa his kingdom, he reads a hilarious edict ordering everyone to eat, drink, dance and make merry for four days. No work is to be done.

Tara cannot understand the need for these four special days; Goans celebrate the Carnaval almost every day anyway.

People have been waiting on barricaded footpaths since 2.30 p.m. Gregory and Tara arrive at the crowded enclosure opposite Old Secretariat by 4.45. The first few floats have begun inching their way down the old Patto Bridge, greeted enthusiastically with shouts of "Viva Carnaval, Viva Goa!" Colourfully attired young men and women precede the floats, singing, dancing, or acting out skits. Their costumes, however, leave a lot to be desired.

Tara has seen one particular style at every Carnaval for the last decade; an A-line maxi with row upon row of frills. Meant to resemble a castanet clicking Spanish dancers' costume, where the bodice is fitted, and the skirt loose and frilly.

At the Goan Carnaval, the slim girls invariably wear XL sizes and the well-endowed ones wear XS. This particular outfit gets passed around every year. One year it will be white with blue frills, then white with green frills, white with red, purple, orange. She imagines mothers and grandmothers awake all night on Carnaval eve, reopening the old frills and replacing them with new ones.

The floats carry their own music – DJs and live bands playing at full amplification, resulting in a cacophony of sounds and music styles. Tara experiences visual fatigue as she counts eight floats on rural Goan life, six showing the famous Goan beach shacks, four on the effects of mining, and two floats on the Andalusia disaster – both depicting only male divers.

"Why only male divers?"

"The common float maker doesn't know there are female divers. Don't take it personally, Tara." Gregory winks.

Tara finds his response rather patronising.

Earlier in the evening, she had refused to sit in the VIP enclosure. "Don't make me sit beside naval aunties in chiffon saris," she'd told him. He did not argue. That stumped her a bit; she was itching for a fight.

Gregory neatly sidestepped her. There's no escaping now, she is stuck to him, all exit points sealed by crowds. A wall of people pushes them from behind, threatening to topple them over. A sea of gaudy absurdity waits in front, to swallow.

The sun sets on the Mandovi in an explosion of colours rivalling the revelry. Nobody seems to notice, being engrossed in the vile painted display. Streetlights come on and as if on cue, the spectators turn boisterous. Jumping over barricades, they rush to join the pretty girls in the parade. Gregory shields Tara with his body. She's irritated, but cannot complain. In the ensuing melee, some chiffon-sari-wearing-naval-aunties faint.

Any sane person would see it as a sign to leave, not Gregory. He wants to stay till the end, or at least till he sees Ocean Fantasy. Knowing her luck, it will be the last float of the parade. Gregory has made plans to take her to dinner, to Vista do Cais. Tara dreads the impending overdose – Vista do Cais Ocean Fantasy Float topped by the Vista do Cais Carnaval Dinner.

Finally Ocean Fantasy starts ambling down the road. Gregory is ecstatic, seeing his idea transformed into reality. A massive glass tank, as large as the truck it's on, is filled with blue water and lit from within. A metre long replica of MV Andalusia bobs and burns inside, threatening to sink as hundreds of tiny men jump off its flaming decks. A huge mermaid sits partially submerged in the tank, helping the men out with her motorised hands. Gregory points to the mermaid and grins, "You!"

"Who?"

"*You*, Tara! Saving the Andalusia sailors!"

She laughs thinking it's one of his jokes.

"Oi, don't like it what?"

A mermaid. She hates mermaids. Pathetic in-betweeners, neither human nor fish. Moving her grossly shaped arms, this one deposits tiny burnt sailors on bystanders. Kids run alongside the float, falling over each other to pick up the burnt GI Joe toys raining on the pavement. Getting into fights over who has collected the most, and who has got the most burnt ones.

Tara continues staring as a sizzling soldier torpedoes her forehead. She is startled. Gregory laughs and starts rubbing her forehead. She cringes at his touch.

Suddenly she is back on the deck of CGS Varuna on a cold February night, surrounded by bodies of charred sailors. But the sailors are all Lilliputian while she is humungous, sleeping amongst them in her sleeping bag. Tara is bewildered. How did she get here?

Just a few minutes ago she was at the Carnaval Float Parade. The deck floor boards groan and strain under her massive body. All of a sudden, the ship deck collapses and she falls through the innards of *CGS Varuna,* making a giant-sized tunnel on her way to the sea. Slowly sinking to the bottom where it is absolutely quiet. Peace at last.

A sharp ringing noise inside her ears shatters the quiet of the sea bed. She opens her eyes, she's back at the carnaval. Getting louder and louder, the ringing reaches a crescendo. Tara opens her mouth to say something.

The tiny sailors from the Andalusia Float start saying her name.

"Tara Tara!"

She looks around. Everybody is waving at her, saying her name. She looks at Gregory for reassurance. His features shift, melt, and re-arrange. So does the rest of his body.

Is she looking through water?

Suddenly the gap between them widens. Gregory is stationary but she's moving away. Tara tries to hold him by his collar, but she's dragged away. In a fish tank.

On a truck. She has become the mermaid. Tara – the papier-mâché mermaid, with grossly misshapen arms. Hauling her body out of the tank, she tries to flee. She falls flat on her face. She has no feet. The tiny soldiers taunt her.

"Tara, Tara, Tara with no feet!"

"Stop saying my name, or I'll scream."

"Tara, Tara, Tara with no feet!"

"Please, just STOP!"

And then it spills out; a blood curdling, stomach churning, eardrum-shattering scream. The crowds, floats, performers – everybody freezes.

Tara continues screaming, "Please, I beg you, stop parading me. Stop!"

She rants and raves. Somebody's hand covers her mouth. She bites it. Turning around, she sees it is attached to Gregory. Ooops! He looks like he's wet his pants. Well, actually, she's wet hers. She's wet all over, having just escaped the fish tank.

Policemen resort to *lathi* charge in a desperate attempt to disperse the crowds, causing a stampede as all exits get blocked. There is complete chaos as the parade gets disrupted. A senior police officer walks over to check on her.

"She's feeling sick. Got pushed around in the crowd," Gregory tells him. "I'll take her to the first aid tent."

"Who are you? How do you know her?" Looking at Tara, he asks, "Is he with you?"

"I'm Captain Gregory Figueiredo, of the Indian Navy." Gregory flashes his ID.

"Pardon me sir, I'll call an ambulance."

"No thanks, we're leaving."

Gregory drags her through the crowd, on a path cleared by the police. People climb over each other to gawk at the fleeing couple. The police hit them with lathis. Tara wants to stay back and help; she would love to gouge all those eyes.

Still dazed, but stable enough to ride pillion, Tara waits patiently as Gregory fetches his bike from the parking lot. Thousands of identical bikes are parked haphazardly. Retrieving one's own requires shifting ten others. He manages to get out of the bike maze and they leave.

The city lights are a million cigarette butts stubbing her eyeballs. She closes her eyes. Darkness is a soothing salve. They pass over the Mandovi Bridge into Porvorim; at the Alto Porvorim roundabout there's a huge traffic jam. Gregory skips the left going to Sangolda and Saligao, and rides towards Guirim. The highway is always sparsely populated on this stretch, picking up traffic near Mapuça. He turns left off the NH-17 near the MRF showroom, taking the narrow field road going towards Parra and Saligao. Near the Piedade Chapel, he screeches to a halt.

She opens her eyes; they have veered off the tarred road and are in the middle of a paddy field. Gregory props his bike on its stand and dismounts, leaving her sitting on it. He takes off his helmet and flings it to the ground, walks a short distance and starts pacing. Suddenly he charges in her direction. Tara almost falls off his bike, cowering at the sight of his raised hand.

"What *was* that?" he barks.

"What?"

"What drama! Everybody was looking at us, you lunatic bitch! Get your head checked, that's if I don't smash it right now."

"*You* designed Ocean Fantasy, you're the lunatic. Get *your* head checked first. How could you do that to me? Parading me as a bloated mermaid. Trivialised the whole tragedy. I can forgive other Andalusia floats, their makers don't know what happened. But *you*? You were there, Gregory. How could you? I'm disgusted."

"You're *disgusted*? I put my heart and soul into that. Why did I even bother? Thought you'd like the float."

"Do you even know what I like?"

The bike roars to life, drowning her voice.

15

Madwoman from the Parade

On Sunday mornings Aajji usually cooks up a feast. Steamed rice cakes dunked in sweet coconut milk, grated coconut and jaggery stuffed inside rice *polas*[12], *Tonachim bhaaji with bhakri, and Ros Omelette.* But today there's just hard *kankhonn*[13] from the *poder*[14].

Tara wonders if the old woman is alright. A quick glance confirms she is fine. But something seems to be eating Aajji.

She eats hurriedly and excuses herself before dad and Aajji can engage her in conversation. Standing in front of the washbasin mirror, she checks her forehead for signs of damage inflicted by the sizzling GI.

There's just a tiny scratch, easily covered by hair. Through the mirror she notices Aajji looking around shifty-eyed. The wash area is hidden from the dining table, but the angled mirror provides Tara a good view of the dining area.

"Is she back in her guest house?" Aajji asks her son.

---

12. rice pancake

13. bangle (Konkani), bangle-shaped bread

14. baker (Konkani, taken from Portuguese Padeiro)

"Must be," he replies. "Left ten minutes ago."

"Good, I have something to tell you."

Tara's dad puts his paper down. "Now what?"

"Your daughter made a scene at the Panjim Carnaval. People are calling her a madwoman."

Tara's dad gets up and shuffles to the refrigerator. Pouring himself a glass of water, he says, "Why those bloody idiots made Andalusia floats? Can't mind their own bloody business? Stick to dancing girls and pretty boys. Why remake a tragedy? Naturally Tara reacted that way. Imagine seeing that whole mess again. Like a bloody recurring nightmare.

"You tell this to everybody – nothing's wrong with my daughter. The float makers are mad. This whole Carnaval stupidity we do every year is mad. Total waste of time and money."

"Baba, just listen to yourself, you sound mad too. Ai Saiba! Everyone's gone mad, am I the only sane person left on earth?"

"Shut up, Aai."

"She was behaving like a possessed woman, they're saying. I think the ghosts of those dead sailors have possessed her."

"Who told you this?"

"No one. I know. I will take care of her now. Our family priest conducts exorcisms. I'm going to speak to him today."

"Don't even think about it, you hear me?"

"Ramesh *putta*[15] stop hiding behind newspapers. You know what's happening in the world, but you have no idea what's happening in your own house. She's a pain from the day she was born."

---

15. Son (Konkani)

"Aai, you never have anything good to say about her. Anyway, it's over and done with."

"It's not! Tomorrow it will be on the front page of *Navhind* and *Herald*...more people will come to know. Grandchildren are supposed to bring joy; she's only brought me misery. If only she could disappear," Aajji mutters.

"Great idea! Tara *does* need to disappear for a while. Anil, my college friend, owns a resort at Ganpatipule. Let's send her there. She can return in a few days when all talk dies down."

"Can she stay there only? There must be a swimming pool no? She can clean it."

"Tara has a good job. Even the navy looks up to her and you want her to clean swimming pools? Illiterate people do that."

"Hope she still has that job when she resumes on Wednesday," says Aajji. "As if what she did in Bombay wasn't bad enough, she had to come here and disgrace herself all over again. Smear cow dung on our Salgaonkar name."

"Aai, we will not discuss *that* topic ever again. Is that clear?"

"Fine! Send her tomorrow, even if it's only for a few days."

Tired of eavesdropping, Tara steps inside the room. "Why tomorrow, I'll go now. Not to any resort. Someplace far away."

"Tara, you're still here, bai, we were just–"

"Aajji, don't bother, I heard everything."

"What did you hear bai? We're just concerned about your behaviour, that's all."

"I'll go away, just like mom. You want me dead, no? Bloated and lifeless like the bodies I fish out? Then I won't get into *any* trouble. I'll be your obedient grandchild. Obedient and dead. That's what you want, no Aajji?"

Aajji is livid. "Ramesh, did you hear? See how she talks. This is the gratitude I get for looking after both of you." Turning to Tara she snaps, "You think I like it when people say bad things about you? It hurts, Tara. I hurt. People are laughing at us in the village, sniggering openly at my face."

Tara is apologetic. "But I didn't do it on purpose, Aajji."

"Of course, you didn't. Imagine if it had happened during Portuguese times. I fear to even think of it."

"What would they have done, cut off my tongue? Bloody barbarians, and they called *us* uncivilised," Tara hisses, her earlier remorse lasting just a few seconds. It's war again.

"Don't talk! You know nothing! They were good for Goa. Look what's happening now – no discipline, no values. Our own children behave in this manner." Aajji wipes a crocodile tear with the corner of her *pallav*.

"Enough of this *tiatr*[16], Tara, go to your house!"

"I'm leaving. And I won't come back ever again."

"Stop being so dramatic, Tara! Just leave the dining room."

Tara packs in less than ten minutes, walks to the main road and waits for a pilot. After fifteen minutes of waiting, she sees Carlos' Fiat down the road and waves out.

"Oh, hi, Tara, I was just coming to your place! Where you off to, with suitcase and all?"

"Holiday."

---

16. Tiatr-drama

"Bai! Bad timing! What about the ball? Don't ditch me last minute!"

"Drop me to the airport." She enters his car and sits beside him.

"Going to Bombay?"

"No."

"Fought with the old woman?" Carlos asks.

"No."

"Then?"

"They don't want me at home," she mumbles.

"Where will you go now?"

"I'll figure something at the airport."

"Rubbish! Just come home with me."

"No."

"Stop being difficult *haan*. Stay with me for a few days. Let them panic and put a missing ad. Then I'll drop you home and claim money from your dad. Good idea no?"

"You're kidnapping me now?" Tara asks.

"Hello? *You* came and sat in my car."

"Fine, I'll stay for a day. Tomorrow I'll go."

⚓

Carlos lives alone. His mother lives in Kuwait with her second husband. Widowed when he was barely a month old, she remarried a much older widower, old enough to be her father.

Carlos's early years were spent in Kuwait, schooling and doing a bit of college. He hated living with his step family. In fact, his two stepbrothers are older than his mother. They constantly picked on him, calling him a loser, and bragging how the mother and son duo were saved by their father.

So when Carlos turned eighteen, he decided to leave Kuwait for good. His mother gave him the keys to his biological father's estate – a large crumbling ancestral house in Parra, and released him to his destiny.

He keeps her suitcase in the guest bedroom and enquires if she's eaten something. When she points to his half-eaten breakfast on the dining table, he explains – "Got sick of that omelette pav. Decided to drive to your house for Aajji's Sunday brunch. But, I had to kidnap you… should've eaten the old lady's food before kidnapping her grandchild, na?" He winks.

"Thanks, Carlos."

"For what, Tara?"

"For letting me stay."

"Come on! Stay as long as you want, Tara. It's your turn. I live at your house practically. Aajji will soon charge me rent."

Tara smiles.

He tries again. "At least *now* tell me what happened."

She takes a deep breath, "Went to a trance party and doped a bit much. Then, at the Carnaval parade I saw the Andalusia Floats and freaked. Don't pretend like you don't know."

"I had no idea, you – it's bad for you, Tara."

"What, the parade or the pot?"

"Drugs! Tara!"

"Oh I only do mild stuff. But at this party there was lots of stuff! No clue what all I had. Anyway, had a horrible trip. Still tripping on and off. I sober up and am high again! Without touching the stuff," she shakes her head in disbelief. "Going mad, I think."

"Bai, just tell me, why you do it? You could get caught, and if Mr Martin gets to know?"

"Mr Martin does *not* need to know."

"Your folks? They know?"

"Maybe. I mean, they never ask, but look, no one can tell. I'm standing *and* talking fine. You, on the other hand, are flat on the floor every time you booze."

"Don't boast," Carlos says angrily. He thought there were no secrets between them. "Yes, I'm an alcoholic, but I have my reasons. What's your problem? You have a loving family and all…"

"You think my life's easy?"

"Bai, nobody's life is easy. I know that. Did you start after Andalusia?"

"No, from college – wait, why you said Andalusia?"

"Hmmm… Andalusia changed you – all of us too – but you most of all, Tara."

"What do you mean?"

"How to say this – don't get mad, ok? After Andalusia you've become *sanku*, you argue all the time, even with Bossman. You work till you're ready to drop. Like… like all that's good and bad in you got magnified – ten times!"

Tara is alarmed. "You're telling me this *now*?"

"How to tell? Bloody hell you behave like you have your period every day!"

Tara gets up and starts pacing. "I've let you down, no?" she asks Carlos. He looks away.

"Don't be like me, Tara. You're so much better…"

"I am just like you…"

Carlos pours a glass of feni for himself. "By the way, you hate Carnaval parades, how come you went?"

"Gregory dragged me."

"Captain Gregory Figueiredo! Isn't navy boy in Cochin?"

"He came for the Carnaval."

"Bai, I know you won't like me saying this, but it doesn't look good, us mixing with them."

"What's this *us* and *them*, we're all divers no? He asked me to come for the parade, so I went."

"If he had asked you for a dance, would you have gone for that too?" Carlos suddenly raises his voice.

"In fact, he *did* ask me, for the Red & Black, and I refused. Told him I always go with you."

"But you're ditching me and running away."

"Can I sleep now? Have to get up early tomorrow."

"Sure, enjoy your siesta. I'll wake you for chai."

"Don't bother! I won't have chai or dinner. Going to sleep right through. Had too many insults today. I'm full man, so full…"

Tara falls into a deep dreamless sleep, missing tea time and dinner just as she had predicted. Long after Carlos has switched off all lights, she awakens to the buzzing of mosquitoes. She gets up and goes to look for a repellent but can't find any in the room. Not wanting to wake up Carlos, she sits on the edge of her bed and looks around.

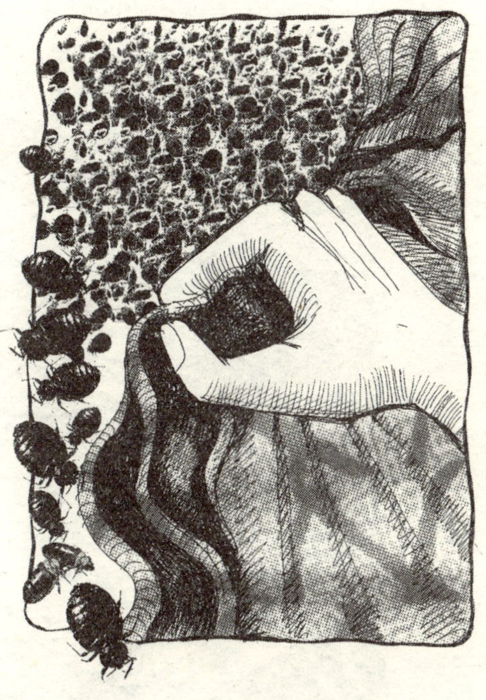

The guest room is threadbare, hardly any furniture and no curtains on windows. A grandfather clock banished to a corner is a mute spectator to passing time. A pair of identical teakwood showcases, covered with cobwebs and dust, display stray pieces of chinoserie. The grand chandelier in the centre of the room does not work; a lone zero-watt bulb is the only source of illumination. But even that is covered with a thick layer of dust. The entire guest room seems to be going to dust. Something inside her snaps. She *has* to clean the bulb. But there's no cloth, no rag – not even curtains she can use. She lifts a corner of her bed cover to wipe it, and almost faints on seeing what lies underneath.

Thousands of bed bugs squirm on a ratty mattress, their shinny black bodies glistening in the dim light. She looks at her arms – tiny red swollen bumps cover them completely. Her feet and stomach aren't spared either.

Horrified, she runs out of the guest room. She wants to burn everything – the mattress, the bed cover, the bed sheet

and her clothes. She looks for Carlos. He is asleep on a couch in the *sala*[17], a bottle of cheap whisky held loosely in one hand, its contents lapped up by the couch. She feels like slapping him awake. *Imagine a bed infested with bed bugs. Does he make his beds at all*, she wonders.

Sitting in a rocking chair, she watches as he sleeps like a child – a very troubled one, albeit. Every few minutes he changes his position, and clutches the bottle tighter; seconds later his grip slackens again. She waits patiently for the bottle to fall; the crash will certainly wake him.

A clock strikes five and Tara opens her eyes. Carlos is sitting beside her bed, staring at her. "Thought you were in a coma or something…"

"What day is it?" She asks, completely disoriented.

"Monday! Bai you slept twenty-four hours straight!"

Tara sits up. The sun is streaming through lace curtains, the grandfather clock is ticking perfectly and the guestroom is spotless. Is this the same dusty room from last night? Did Carlos clean it while she was asleep? She lifts the bed cover to check for bugs. Carlos looks at her questioningly, "What?"

"Weren't there – no, nothing!"

"Tara, stay as long as you wish, I won't tell your folks – I swear. Just chill, watch TV, sleep for two days at a stretch … your folks will think you're on your holiday. You'll save money also."

---

17. Hall

"Doesn't make sense!" she replies, checking her arms. There are no traces of last night's bug bites.

"It makes perfect sense. Tomorrow is the Red & Black. Don't ditch me Tara."

"I'm not carrying any party clothes."

"I'll arrange something, Tara."

Next day Tara opens her suitcase and sees her new red dress right on top. It was hanging in her wardrobe – its plastic covering and price tag still on – when she left home two days ago. But she can no longer trust her memory. She wears it and calls out to Carlos. "Do you have something black I can wear? A jacket, scarf or gloves?"

He walks into her room looking rakish like a mafia don. Teaming an all black three-piece suit with a red cravat and a red hat. He has gelled his mop of curls to make them behave. Not much help that, they just look springier and shinier. Placing a black beret jauntily on her head, he says it's time to leave.

They make quite an impression at the ball. People stare shamelessly. "You look gorgeous," Carlos whispers. But Tara hears something else.

Look! It's the madwoman from the parade!

16

Beating a Retreat

Tara makes it to the front-page of *Gomantak Times*, *Navhind Times* and *O Heraldo*. The only saving grace – everything is reported out of context.

One headline says, 'Woman disturbed by the quality of this year's floats.' Journalists have interpreted her showdown to suit their own agendas. The reports are scathing critiques on the falling aesthetic standards of Carnaval floats. Ocean Fantasy is singled out for being insensitive and the ugliest of the lot.

Speculating on the identity of the hysterical woman, one newspaper wonders if she's a wife or a girlfriend of a dead sailor from *MV Andalusia*. Captain Gregory Figueiredo and Chef Benny Da Costa are the only names mentioned, being the float designer and promoter.

The madwoman is nameless and faceless. All pictures focus on her back (she wore her red sequinned halter top that day). Low angle camera shots show a distorted Ocean Fantasy as seen from the madwoman's perspective.

Tara is thrilled. Ocean Fantasy deserves to be shredded. Public outrage is the best way to nip Gregory's float designing career in the bud. Before bigger monstrosities are thrust upon all and sundry. As soon as she steps into office, Mr Martin pops out of his cabin and calls her. Tara takes a deep breath, enters his cabin and closes the door behind her. He has already ordered sandwiches and tea for two. "Sit down," he commands. "Eat something."

"I had breakfast, thank you."

"How you feeling, Tara?"

"Fine."

He stares at her, gathering his thoughts. "Tara, everyone's blaming me."

"What you talking about, Mr Martin?"

"The float parade," he stops and sips his tea. "Searching for dead bodies has taken a toll on you. You saw a replica of Andalusia and freaked out. Everyone had warned me, it's not a woman's job. I didn't listen – why you smiling?"

"Team up with my Aajji. She thinks I'm possessed," says Tara beaming from ear to ear.

"Come on Tara, I'm sure Aajji doesn't think that."

"She does! And not just any possession. Dead Andalusia sailors!"

"Tara, these things happen – panic attacks, nightmares, PTSD they're calling it now – it's part of our lives. We risk dying every day, forgodsakes. Rest of the time we're handling dead bodies. I've done this longer than you. I've had my bad moments too. But never have I ever single-handedly stopped a Carnaval!" he says and lets out a roaring belly laugh.

"Oh boy! You are one crazy woman! You've done what nobody could do, stopped the fucking Goa Carnaval!"

Tara joins him for a few minutes of hysterical laughter, the kind that stops and restarts, with tears flowing freely. It's just the cathartic release she needs.

Getting serious, he says, "But Tara, accept that you have a problem. See a counsellor, just someone to talk to. Take some anxiety medication. No big deal, it's covered by your medical."

"Mr Martin, it was nothing! I saw that stupid float and I snapped. I'm fine now," she says. "And what's this woman's job nonsense? Never thought you'd talk like this. *You*, Mr Martin?"

"Tara, you're fine now. How long before you crack again? Before you go all loony, seek help." Realising he's been a bit harsh, he softens his stand. "Okay fine, if you don't want to see a counsellor, at least take a break. I'm sanctioning you three months paid leave. Here, take the keys to our company guest house. It's on Colva Beach. Sometimes rest is all you need. Rest works wonders for one's mental health."

"A company guest house? Martins' Dredging has a company guest house? You've been hiding it for how long?"

"Not hiding it, my dear. Company guest house only for tax purposes. It's my holiday home. I'm doing you a favour. Be grateful."

"No, thanks!"

"Look, you have three months leave piled up. Don't let it lapse. Normally I don't care. I mean, an employee can only encash their leaves if they're quitting…"

"Three months sounds like maternity leave." She makes a face saying it.

"Tara, if you need maternity leave this year itself, I will give it to you. Don't worry dear, it's the law."

"Haha, very funny. But I'd like to make my own plans. No Colva."

"I'm just giving you a choice," Mr Martin says to her and leaves it at that.

Tara was expecting to get fired but got a bonus instead. She runs to give Carlos the good news.

"Damn it, Tara, can't you see what he's done?"

"He's given me a three month, all-expenses paid, holiday-cum-sick leave. Great *na*?"

"Bai, can't you see the catch?"

"What catch?"

"Stupid girl, by the time you return – nicely tanned all over – you'll have no job."

"Rubbish!"

"He's going to replace you!"

"Replace *me*? With whom?"

"Your float parade boy," Carlos sniggers.

"Shut up Carlos! Don't talk nonsense. Why would Gregory leave the navy? And join us? Martins' of all people."

"Yes, *us!* Martins'!"

"Impossible! Gregory hates this place. In fact, he was advising *me* to leave."

"Obviously, he's had an eye on your job."

"Anything you talk, why would he eye a sweeper's job?" Tara sounds irritated.

"*Why?* Mr Martin is paying him three times what navy pays, *that's why*."

Tara looks around if someone else will corroborate Carlos. Nobody wants to meet her gaze. She goes to the divers' room and sits on the floor, leaning against the wardrobe. "Please move, Tara. Let me get my wetsuit," says Cajetan, forcing her to shift position. At 5.30 p.m., she gets up and leaves. In her ten years at Martins', she has never left so early without doing any work.

Tara reaches the Panjim bridge junction smack in the middle of evening rush hour. The vehicles waiting to get on the bridges are moving at a snail's pace. She takes a detour to Bambolim and decides to ride into the city from the Dona Paula and Miramar side. At Miramar Beach, she almost parks her scooter in the parking lot near Miramar Residency, but changes her mind seeing the crowd. Going further, she enters into Kala Academy, and heads to the canteen. Picking up a plate of *samosas,* she walks to the beach.

She sits on a steel bench facing the lighthouse and stares vacantly at the horizon. The samosas fall off her tilted paper plate. A few stray dogs loitering on the rocks get into a fight while trying to steal the food.

Tara intervenes and starts feeding them individually. Seeing the commotion, a security guard walks up to her and admonishes her for feeding strays. She gets up and leaves.

Back on the road, she veers into the inside lanes of Fontainhas. Two of her diver colleagues, Cajetan and Tony, live here. She does not want their families to see her; they'll be sitting in their balcãos. Taking the Old Patto bridge back into Panjim, she rides around the Old Secretariat, Abbe Faria statue, Menezes Braganza Institute, Municipal Market, over and over again. She can't go home either; there's a cold war brewing.

Aajji was watching last night when Carlos dropped her. Strangely, no questions were asked at today morning's breakfast. Not a good sign at all. Tara feels a lot better when they have their spats; at least she knows what's on Aajji's mind.

Window-shopping is the only alternative left. If she's being exiled to the company guest house, the least she can do is go there in style. Boutiques and arcades are aplenty in the star hotels scattered all over Panjim. Peeping into a shop window, she sees a collection of swimwear and summer wear at a 50 % discount sale.

Tara has the best swimsuits money can buy, and she has enough. But her entire collection is the no-nonsense variety, engineered for minimum drag in water, with just the right percentage of Neoprene and Lycra. Nothing like the swimsuits most women prefer – floral, frilly and stringy thingies. She wears hers to work, like a uniform.

She tries a fluorescent green bikini. Not bad at all; black isn't the only colour that becomes her. She picks up some Hawaiian print shorts and tank tops along with the bikini. Paying for her purchases, she is certain they'll go to the lowest section of her wardrobe. And stay there until repurposed as donated clothes.

Her folks see nothing amiss when she walks in for dinner at 9.30 p.m. Eating at a furious pace, Tara avoids their gaze. She is about to excuse herself, when the old nag opens her mouth. "Is this a hotel, Tara? Do you see a board outside – *Aajji's Hotel. Free food for useless grandchildren*? Where were you for four days?"

"At a friend's."

"Which one?" Aajji asks.

"None of your business."

Her dad deliberately stays out of these fights. 'Grandmother-Granddaughter Tiatr Company' he has dubbed them, having suffered every show from his dress circle seat for the last ten years.

"Let her go, Aai," he says. "Tara told me. I only didn't tell you. You were in a bad mood."

Tara scoots before Aajji can retort.

Back in her house, she's about to put out the lights when her mobile rings for the first time in the day.

"Didn't go to Cochin?" she asks.

"Calling from there only,"

"Ok."

"Oi, still mad at me wot?"

"Just mad," she replies and is not amused when he guffaws.

"Got to tell you something…"

"I know, you're leaving the navy."

There is a brief silence. And then, Gregory asks, "Who told you?"

"And I know where you're joining."

"Oh, Mr Martin told you!" he says cheerfully, "I wanted to surprise you, so I had requested him not to tell…"

"Listen Gregory, spare me your surprises, okay? They give me nightmares."

After a pause Gregory says, "I don't understand."

"Don't pretend like you don't know. You saw me ill and swooped on my job," she yells. "Why! You don't even like Martins'. Goddammit, you were asking *me* to leave. Now, I know why, bloody vulture!"

"Calm down, Tara! I'm not swooping on *anyone's* job. Mr Martin begged me to join. He made me a fantastic offer. He said you're overworked and you need someone to share your load. Of course, I'll be senior to you. After all, I'm from the navy and..."

"That's not what I heard."

"Mr Martin said he's sanctioned you three months sick leave. He's worried about you, Tara. We all are. Take the vacation; do yourself a favour, Tara."

"How can I? I'll be fired when I return."

"What? Who told you this?"

"Carlos."

"Dammit," Gregory sounds exasperated. "Why do you listen to that bugger! Bloody gossip he is. Listen, Tara, your dear friend Carlos will get *his* ass fired if he doesn't perform. There are plenty of hard working and deserving divers in the navy; they could definitely use the money..."

Gregory hasn't even joined and already he's talking like he owns Martin's Dredging.

Tara imagines Mr Martin sitting in a stall at the Saturday Night Market, under a board saying – 'Diving Lessons! Rs 500 per dive'. And Carlos? In a stall opposite, his board saying – 'Dancing Lessons! Rs 10 per lesson'. Midway through the night, Carlos gets up, strikes out the number ten and makes it rupees five. That's enough for a glass of feni at his local bar.

"Oi, Tara...fell asleep or wot?"

"Listening..."

"What will you do in Colva? Oldies go there."

"I'll find a sugar daddy."

"You're joking, right?"

"I'm dead serious."

"Ok-ok, just get well. I'll come and entertain you if you get bored."

"Good night Gregory." Tara disconnects the call.

She is bewildered at the plotting going on behind her back. Everybody knew; only she had no clue. Maybe she really does need to go to Colva, away from Martins' Dredging, away from Carlos, from Gregory, from Aajji, her dad. Mr Martin was right; she needs a break from people.

Just commune with the sea and the fish. But so much free time! Two thousand one hundred and sixty hours! What will she do, stare at the ceiling?

Tara falls asleep, dreaming of an old woman wearing a bikini and prancing in the blue-green waters of a secluded beach.

17

Crematorium View Apartments

Tara wakes up in a cold sweat. Her dad is knocking on her bedroom window. She slides it open; it's morning.

"No office today?"

"I'm on leave Dad, forgot to tell you last night."

"Leave or time off?"

"Leave."

"Ok, listen Tara, there's some bad news."

"Office called? Some emergency?" she perks up.

"No, Ameeta *maushi* died."

"Oh." Ameeta maushi is her mother's older unmarried sister.

"She had cancer. You'll have to go for the funeral."

"No way!"

"Tara, one should forgive and forget. Whatever happened is in the past. Besides, don't you miss Bombay? The cremation is tomorrow, take the afternoon flight – I'll pay. And Tara, be civil with everyone, okay? Don't argue, no matter what they say. Keep your mouth shut, okay?"

"Do they think I'm responsible for her death too?"

"Don't be silly."

"But Dad…"

"Just do it bai."

⚓

On arrival in Bombay, Tara heads straight to her mother's maternal home, near Opera House, Grant Road. She does the rounds, meeting relatives not seen or spoken to in decades. Picking an opportune moment she slips out, deciding to return later. In any case, the idea of roaming the city at night, after all these years, is far more appealing. She hails a taxi and goes to the suburbs.

An aged Punjabi couple lives in their third floor apartment in Versova, Andheri. In Bombay, the resale value of an apartment nosedives when an occupant commits suicide, or if a child dies, or if there's been a murder on the premises. The apartment is considered inauspicious; nobody will have it even for free. These folks, then in their late fifties, were desperate perhaps. Besides, after her mother died, Dad was in a hurry to leave Bombay, so he sold it way below market rates.

Tara rings the doorbell and reintroduces herself. They invite her in for a cup of tea, and she gets a chance to reminisce. She has always called it, 'Crematorium View Apartments', never 'Ocean View Apartments', its real name.

The expensive flats are sea-facing, the less expensive ones face a Hindu crematorium. It was recently converted to an electric one, the old couple inform her. Anyone seeing it for the first time will think it's a factory for processing the dead.

⚓

When Tara lived here, the crematorium used the traditional sandalwood and fire method. Her favourite pastime in those days was to guess the age of a burning body. She did this by sniffing the acrid smoke billowing out. If the wind decided to blow their way, her mother's vegetable pulao would smell like mutton biryani. (In Saligao, her grandmother's mutton biryani sometimes smells and tastes like vegetable pulao.)

When it was a young body on the pyre, the smoke made her eyes water like she had bitten a green chilli. The entire house smelled of chicken tandoori. With an older body, the tears just wouldn't stop. The smoke, like a mean onion, made her cry non-stop. The aroma was of a Mutton Xacuti left outside the refrigerator all night, by mistake, that too in the middle of a May heat wave. Rancid meat!

It happened once, when her parents went to Goa. Tara was in college, old enough to fend for herself. Yet her mother cooked food for two weeks and stored it in the refrigerator in melamine containers. A mutton curry was left out to cool on the kitchen counter. Tara was asked to refrigerate it – she forgot.

Two days later she discovered her mistake and tentatively lifted the lid.

Baaaadooom! The entire room filled with a familiar smell. That day the crematorium came home.

She stands in her old balcony, watching kids clambering up and down the massive entrance gate. The main gate opens only for taxis and cars. People have to use a smaller one on its side. She could recognize the peculiar squeaking of the iron gates even in her sleep. It symbolised returning home, or going on vacation, when it opened wide to let in or let out their luggage-laden taxi.

Tara's childhood involved a lot of travelling, mostly between Bombay and Goa, their two homes in those days. It was quite disorienting for a child; to sleep in Bombay and wake up in Goa, and vice-versa. Later, as a teenager, she embarked on other expeditions. Again, between Bombay and Goa. Till that fateful day when Bombay shut its doors on her, leaving her stranded forever, in Goa. That day she stood at her front door, straining to look above the heads of people blocking her path. Aware of a dull pain in her uterus. She had not felt it in college, engrossed in answering her last exam. It throbbed in unison with her heartbeat. Ameeta maushi spotted her. She dragged Tara inside the living room and pointed to the floor, "Look what you've done!" Tara saw a body on the floor, covered with a blood-soaked white sheet. Her mom's favourite *samai*[18] was lit beside it.

---

18. metal lamp on a pedestal with several wicks

Finding white-sheet-covered-bodies on their living room floor was not unusual for Tara. Since they lived opposite a Hindu crematorium, relatives and family friends on deathbed were often brought to their house to die. It was purely a matter of convenience for everybody. Tara rarely shed tears on such occasions.

"Why have you used Mom's samai? She'll get back from work and scold me! I'll get the smaller one. Mom's samai is for her time..." Just then, Tara saw her dad among the mourners, looking sadder than the occasion demanded.

This indiscriminate lending of their home for funerals was taking a toll on her family. Tara made a mental note to talk to both parents – but later, after everyone had dispersed. "Who died?" Tara asked Dad. That's when Ameeta maushi lost it. Rushing to Tara, she caught hold of her hair and dragged her. Banging her forehead on the floor beside the white-sheet-covered body, she screamed, "You murderer! Your Mom died!"

What did maushi say? A murderer? Was there a murderer on the loose? Had he murdered her mom? Wait, Ameeta maushi called her a murderer.

Dad held her tight, to stop her screaming. Her mother's body lay broken in a hundred different places; her beautiful face smashed beyond recognition. A suicide note was displayed prominently for everyone to read. Thanks to Ameeta maushi.

Three days before all of this, Tara had mustered enough courage to disclose her pregnancy to both parents. Dad had looked pleadingly, hoping it was a prank. When he realised it wasn't, he became silent. Tara saw it as a good sign; it meant he considered her an adult. And she was! She was twenty-two.

Emboldened, she broached the topic of abortion, promising she would never attend another rave party in Goa, for as long as she lived.

"Is he your classmate," her Dad had asked.

"No, just someone I met."

"Stranger?" her Dad asked, aghast.

"Not exactly, but no one from our family knows him. It's good, news won't spread."

"Have you told him you're pregnant, and you're going to abort?"

"I shouldn't bother him with such things, he's busy..."

Her mother had got really mad at this point, "Busy? He bloody well take responsibility. Which young boy from a decent family gets a girl pregnant? Both of you are at fault. Bloody fools, both of you."

And then Tara was forced to divulge more details – details she wished to withhold.

"He's not young exactly," she had hesitated. "He's a foreigner, a musician – but he's living in Goa for many many years."

"What's his name, how old is he?" her Dad had interrupted.

"Must be forty-five or fifty-five..."

"What?" Her dad was livid. "I am going to the police. Who does he think he is? Is he running a sex racket? Drugging young Indian girls and sleeping with them?"

Tara wanted her parents to understand she wasn't a victim, nor was anyone the perpetrator. In tears she had confessed, "It's my fault entirely. He's a respected man. People call him Bholenath Guruji in the music circles..."

Suddenly her mother's composure crumpled. Tara had seen her cry on several occasions, but never so pitifully. "Please don't cry, Mummy. I'm really sorry..."

Her mother continued bawling, "This is so wrong! Tara, how could you? How could you hurt me like this?" Alternating it with threats, "I'm going to kill you, I won't let you get away with this."

Her father meanwhile had snapped out of his stupor. "It's okay. We can handle this. It's not the end of the world. Look at Tara, look how sorry she is. She has realised her mistake. It doesn't look good if we lose control like this. She depends on us for support."

Tara watched her mother rage silently for the next three days. She did not go to work, cook for the family, or eat. Just locked herself in her room. And then, after three days had passed, she snapped out of her funk. As if nothing had happened. As if she had erased the entire episode from her memory.

Her mother had woken up early that day, cooked breakfast for everybody and dressed for office. Tara was relieved; she decided to get the abortion.

After Tara and dad left the house, Mrs Sukanya Salgaonkar carefully bolted all doors and windows – like she had always done before leaving for office. Put the house keys in her handbag. She opened the bar cabinet and took out the bottle of Laphroaig that Tara's dad had been saving for her graduation. Drinking it neat as she climbed four flights of stairs to the terrace of their seven storey building. And she jumped.

There was so much blood on the papads left out to dry by Mrs Mhatre of ground floor.

18

Ms Kamath and Mr Harrison

Before she got married and became a Salgaonkar, Sukanya was a Kamath. She lived near Opera House on Grant Road. Schooling and attending college in South Bombay, she had never stepped inside a local train, Western or Central. Her father's white Ambassador dropped her everywhere. When she turned eighteen, he gifted her a white Volkswagen Beetle. Being the younger of two daughters, she was pampered by both parents.

The advantages of being young in Bombay of the seventies were many. South Bombay was where all the action was. Sukanya and her friends partied at Studio 29 and attended protests at Cross Maidan. It was a carefree life, attending college at St. Xavier's, watching movies at Metro and Eros, and shopping on Colaba Causeway.

One morning Sukanya received a phone call that would change the course of her life. Leslie, her college mate, was speaking gibberish. Junior to her by a couple of years, he had this habit of speaking really fast.

"GeorgeHarrisonisbaskingonthebeachoutsidemyhouse inCalangute."

"Lez, speak slowly."

"George Harrison is basking on the beach outside my house in Calangute."

"Are you serious?"

"My Nana just called… I'm thinking, why don't we go and check him out?""

"I'll have to ask my dad."

"Ok. I'll check if restofthegang wants to come."

"Yes please, Dad won't let me go alone with you."

George Harrison was in Goa, lazing on Calangute Beach like any ordinary hippie. How crazy was that! He had released his Wonderwall album in Bombay when Sukanya was just a baby. Two decades and several albums later, he was back in India, this time in Goa. As an anonymous beachcomber he would be as equal as any man lying on a beach mat.

Leslie called again; the only tickets available were on the lowest deck of the passenger liner Konkan Sevak. They decided to take her Beetle and drive in turns. Four youngsters patiently heard their parents lecture them on driving safely, on the six-hundred-kilometre stretch of National Highway No 17.

"Will he still be there tomorrow?" asked Pooja. "What if he leaves before we arrive?"

"My neighbour, who has a taverna on the beach, is plying him with food and drinks. He said Georgie will stay for a month."

"Ask him to mix some hash golis in his drink," said Sukanya, "it will be impossible to catch any flight."

"Kiddos, why do you think he's come to Goa? For *sheeth-kodi*[19]?" asked Leslie, dripping sarcasm. "He's flying already, no airplane required!"

"What to do when we meet him?" asked Pravin.

Leslie pondered for a minute, "Let's see! I'll ask him to perform at the college festival. I'll make him sign two hundred autographs, and sell them for hundred rupees each. If he's too stoned, I'll take thumb impressions, but those will fetch only fifty rupees."

"Wow Lez, I don't think he'll ever come back to India…" said Sukanya, the oldest in the group.

Cracking jokes to stay awake, they kept a steady stream of banter flowing till they crossed the Sawantwadi border into Goa at 4 a.m. next morning. In another hour, they were at Calangute village. Heading straight to the beach, they looked for Mr Harrison. Of course he wasn't there; not a soul on the dark beach. It would be sun up at 6.30 a.m. Trooping inside Leslie's ancestral house, they went to sleep.

Sukanya woke up and parted the window curtains above her bed. The sight unfolding before her eyes was unbelievable.

---

19. Rice and curry (in Konkani)

Calangute beach stretched beyond her window, with row upon row of bodies glistening in the sun. Looking for Georgie amidst this mass of flesh would be impossible. On the balcão, the boys were already on the lookout, armed with binoculars.

"Is that him?"

"No, thatpaunchistoobigmen."

"Look! *George Harrison*!"

"Bugger, wrong again!"

"Boys," Sukanya interrupted, "you need to change your strategy."

They turned around to look, not having noticed her arrival in their midst.

"Sitting here with binocs isn't going to help. I see two options. We form pairs and comb the beach, or…"

"Or?" asked Pravin.

"Find someone who knows, like a reporter, tour guide, or a bartender."

"No way I'm stepping out," said Pooja. "Too sunny. Don't want to become dark."

"Anyone else for staying indoors?" asked Leslie.

"Not me," said Sukanya, getting up and letting her bathrobe drop to the floor. She was wearing a red bikini.

"Who's George Harrison?" asked Leslie, looking at Sukanya. "Sukanya, follow me to my room. And the rest of you can go look for whatever his name is."

"Oh come on, stop teasing!" Sukanya blushed to the shade of her bikini.

Running on the hot sand, she headed straight for the waves. "I'll be the first to find him."

George Harrison was forgotten. They spent the entire day drinking beer and getting roasted in the sun. Taking a break in the afternoon, they had lunch on the balcão and headed right back to the beach. Even Pooja was coaxed out; Leslie told her that feni worked like a sun block when applied on bare skin. The pairs were formed by default that day: Pooja and Pravin, Leslie and Sukanya.

Rest of the week passed with the couples going their separate ways, and regrouping at night to discuss the day's exploits. Everybody wholeheartedly agreed that George Harrison had unwittingly become a good excuse to have fun in Goa. Soon the last few days of their stay were around the corner. Two weeks had passed like two hours.

On their last day, Sukanya and Leslie packed their bags in the morning and decided to give 'Mission George Harrison' one last try. They found an empty spot beside a guitar-strumming hippie, and settled down spreading their beach mats. He was an over-friendly sort, regaling them with songs and stories of his exploits in the country. They were relieved that their journey, undertaken in search of a musical prodigy, was at least ending to the strains of his songs. So what if someone else was doing the singing. And doing a damn good job too!

"Are you a famous musician?"

"Not yet."

"But you are so good!" Sukanya gushed.

Graciously accepting her compliments, he continued serenading her. Playing two pieces in a loop, till Leslie got irritated and asked him to stop.

"Please continue," Sukanya said sweetly. "Be grateful he's entertaining us," she whispered to Leslie.

"He's making a pass at you," Leslie remarked, loud enough for the hippie to hear. "Can't you understand, he is playing 'Red Lady too' and 'Love Scene' repeatedly."

"Oh don't be ridiculous. Just a coincidence, is it not?" she asked the hippie, who had heard the entire conversation.

"Pure coincidence!" he said, and winked at her.

Sukanya blushed, irritating Leslie further. He stood up, rolled his beach mat in a huff and stomped off, leaving her alone with the hippie.

"Why are you in Goa?" the hippie asked Sukanya.

"We're a group of four friends from Bombay. We've come here to meet George Harrison. Somebody told us he's on Calangute beach," she said sheepishly.

"So, did you meet him?"

"Is he really here?" Sukanya turned around and looked in all directions. "Where? We've looked everywhere!"

"Not on the beach at the moment. He's staying in a villa with me and my friends."

"He is staying with you!?" Sukanya could barely conceal her excitement.

"Yes," said the hippie, "and he would have occupied the space your beautiful body is occupying right now. But he woke up this morning with a migraine – thank god for that."

"No way!"

"This is his guitar. See, his signature's on it."

"Wow! Can I touch?" Sukanya asked excitedly.

"Strum it," he said. "I won't tell. Not that he'd mind…"

"Please, can I meet him?" she asked, "but only if he's feeling fine."

"He'd love to meet you, miss…er?"

"Sukanya."

"I'm Richard, nice to meet you, Sukanya. By the way, my Indian friends call me Bhole, short for Bholenath. You can call me whatever you want."

Sukanya was ecstatic with her serendipitous encounter. Richard-aka-Bholenath was so charming and mature in comparison to her friends. Rolling up their mats, they walked to a villa exactly three houses away from Leslie's. Sukanya could not believe her friends and she had searched high and low for George Harrison, and all the while he was holed up right under their noses. Stepping inside Richard's house, they learnt that George had gone to Panjim to see a doctor. She decided to wait. In any case, Leslie's ancestral house was only a few metres away.

"Can I get you something to drink?" Richard asked her.

"I'm fine."

"A smoke?"

"No, thanks. We're leaving for Bombay in a few hours. I'll be driving – we'll drive in turns, but – okay, nothing too strong."

"Sure."

She sat in the veranda, smoking weed and waiting. Richard lay in a hammock close by, chattering endlessly. He fell silent after a while.

"The mosquitoes are feasting on you, Sukanya."

She had nodded off, dazed and tired by a whole day in the sun. All she wanted was to take off her sweaty bikini and stand under a cold shower. Richard stepped out of his hammock and walked towards her. "Would you like to go inside and wait?" he asked.

She looked at him, feeling drained. "I'm so tired, I can barely stand."

"Let me help you," he said and lifted her in his arms.

Resting her head on his shoulders, she burrowed her face into his dreadlocks. He kissed her gently and took her to his room. All Sukanya could remember of their languid encounter was the way he devoured her with his piercing grey-green eyes. The feel of his coarse dreadlocks against her skin, and the fragrance of sandalwood that permeated through it all would remain with her for years to come.

Sukanya woke up at 7.30 p.m. Her friends would be combing the beach by now, looking for her. She had to leave. Richard kissed her tenderly on her lips, apologising for being unable to introduce her to her idol.

"Actually, I don't even like him," she said. "You are a better musician, Richard." Lingering a few seconds longer, she looked at him, and ran off to join her friends.

"There she is!" cried Pooja, loading luggage into the car. "Where were you? We looked everywhere."

"I was around…"

"You won't believe what happened after I left you with that hippie," said Leslie, no longer angry with her.

Pooja rolled her eyes. "He has repeated that story at least fifty times."

"I was very pissed off, you know, with you and that guitar-playing-bugger. So I went home, changed, and left for Panjim," said Leslie to Sukanya. "I picked up wine and cashew packets, and then stopped at a chemist and guess who was standing beside me?"

"GEORGE HARRISON!" screamed everyone.

"Thank goodness, at least one of us saw him," said Sukanya. "Did you invite him for the college fest? Did he give you two hundred autographs?

"Mad or wot? He's not my uncle."

"Autographs?"

"Got one each for all of us."

"*Bas*?" Sukanya asked.

"Arrey, at least I managed this much. What did you do? Bet you doped with that hippie bugger."

"Long story short, the hippie, called Richard aka Bholenath, turned out to be a friend of George Harrison who was staying at his place. I went to their villa – just three houses from here – and waited for Harrison to show up. How was I to know that Leslie had detained him at a chemist shop, to sign autographs? I waited and waited, and finally gave up."

"Just four autographs, Sukanya, and I'm not giving you yours. You've been very mean to me today."

"Don't want it; I got something better. I played his guitar."

"Liar."

"I swear."

"Fine, but no one will believe you. See, I have autographs – solid proof."

"Girls and boys, stop fighting. Let's go home," said Pravin.

In a few days, Sukanya would start her first job at a bank. She would have to dress conservatively and be on her best behaviour. These last two weeks in Goa were pure freedom.

Driving through the palm-tree-lined winding roads, she felt sad leaving it all behind. Especially Richard. She continued driving, lost in her thoughts. Not seeing the young man crossing at the crossroad near Mae de Deus Church, Saligao.

19

Chance Encounter

They rushed the young man to Asilo hospital in Mapuça. Ramesh Salgaonkar suffered a fracture in his left femur; he was in a lot of pain. The doctors said he would need crutches for two months. Regretting the accident caused by her daydreaming at the wheel, Sukanya decided to stay back in Goa. She called her dad and arranged all expenses for his treatment, and also handled the police formalities. Her three friends continued their journey by bus the next day.

Sukanya dropped Ramesh home after he was discharged. All of Saligao had assembled outside his house to receive him. His mother stood ahead of the crowd, happy to see her son, but showing no sympathy for Sukanya. Who could blame her? Her son was leaning on crutches, besotted by the rich city girl who had landed him in that position. It did not augur well at all.

Ramesh took Sukanya around his Saligao estate, giving her a tour of his orchards. He told her it was his dream to set up a small office in Bombay. The wholesale fruit markets were massive; business worth lakhs was made by the hour in Bombay. Nearly all his clients – the five-star hotels – were headquartered there.

The city was worth a try. He was confident his fruit business would flourish there.

"My dad knows important people; he can help you with licences and stuff."

"Thanks Sukanya, I don't want to trouble you or your dad."

"Ramesh, I owe you at least this much."

"You owe me nothing. Someone else would've left me to die."

"Okay, then at least call me when you come to Bombay. I can take you sightseeing. You know, so many new discos have opened in Bombay!"

"Never been to a disco," he admitted sheepishly.

"You must come then, when you're okay to dance."

Two weeks after Sukanya Kamath left Goa, Ramesh moved to Bombay. He was advised to rest his leg for two months, but he was in a hurry to walk. Dance, rather. His impatience gave him a permanent limp in his left leg. Just a slight one, like a shuffle. Like someone dragging his foot because of a snapped sandal strap.

Exactly two months after the accident, Ramesh married the woman who caused it. And set up office in Bombay. His mother objected to both decisions, but he paid no heed.

Stretched out on the Mae de Deus crossroad that beautiful evening, he had experienced an epiphany. Bending over him was the woman he was going to marry. Ramesh smiled at her – it was an idiotic smile. His trousers were torn and a bone was sticking out. Blood collected in a pool around his body. The woman was crying, her tears streaking his face as she leaned close. But he was smiling. And then, the euphoria disappeared, as quickly as it had waltzed into his body, replaced by a horrible, shooting pain.

Life presents opportunities disguised as chance encounters. Ramesh Salgaonkar felt fortunate to have recognised his. So he took two chances simultaneously, one with Bombay, the other with a Bombay woman.

Winning Sukanya's hand was the easier part. Starting over in Bombay was easier said than done. His house in Saligao and his mother – who would now be living alone – had to be looked after. But he had good neighbours; they promised to check on her every day.

Sukanya, meanwhile, had started well in her bank job. Taking advantage of the home-loan schemes offered to employees, they bought an apartment in Versova, a faraway suburb of Bombay. Their first and only child, a girl, was born seven months into marriage. In spite of being premature, she was healthy and looked fully developed. They thanked their lucky stars and named her Tara. She had grey-green eyes.

20

The Family Temple

Tara returns home after her aunt's cremation in Bombay, in time for *Shigmo* and her birthday, both on 20 March.

March is always a disgusting month. Everything happens only in the month of March. Carnaval, Lent, Shigmo, Holi, HSC exams, SSC Exams, her birthday – everything piles up, causing a stampede, as events overlap each other. It's a crazy month for all, but especially in Goa. The two principal communities, Catholics and Hindus, do their best to outdo each other at going insane, all within the space of a few weeks.

Aajji likes to attend *zatras* that take place during Shigmo – the Hindu version of Carnaval. Zatras are village fairs held in honour of a temple deity. All night plays, folk songs, folk dances, and magic shows are conducted on an open ground adjoining the temple. Jugglers, fire-eaters and theatre artists from far-flung villages come and perform for a few nights only. There's one particular zatra that Aajji unfailingly attends every year – the *Shirgao* zatra in Bicholim. When Tara came to live in Saligao, she took over from dad the responsibility of escorting Aajji.

As a child, Tara considered the Shirgao zatra a chapter come alive from Arabian Nights. Colourfully attired Dhond tribals wearing wristbands of jasmine flowers danced all night to frantic beating of drums and cymbals. Tents around the perimeter sold plastic toys, steel utensils, jaggery sweets, candy floss, laminated prints of gods and goddesses, and ready-made clothes. Laden thick with religious fervour, the night breeze fanned a huge bonfire in the centre of the ground.

Carlos arrives to usher in Tara's birthday at midnight. On learning about their zatra plans, he begs to join them. Aajji happily agrees seeing that he's got his car. They leave after dinner.

"You know, Carlos, Shirgao zatra is about self confidence." Tara says, seated beside him. Aajji is in the backseat, looking out the window. Tara continues, "Confidence building workshops make people walk on burning coals nowadays. Let's tell Mr Martin to have one for us, what say?"

"You gone mad or what? As it is we kill ourselves at work, you want us to walk on burning coals now?"

"Arrey, anyone can do it. Ash formed on top of coals absorbs the heat, that's why feet don't get burnt. But you have to run fast, there's a technique to doing it right. It's *really* no big deal."

"What rubbish are you talking, Tara?" Aajji scolds her, "Only those who have strong faith in Goddess Lairai can walk on burning coals. The Dhonds dance around the bonfire chanting her name in a trance, till she enters their body and gives them strength to walk on hot coals." Aajji gives Carlos the religious perspective.

At Bicholim, the road is blocked with devotees and onlookers. The devotees headed to the Lairai temple are all dressed in red dhotis, vividly coloured scarves lined with zari borders thrown over their shoulders. They will circumambulate a huge bonfire, holding a stick made of twisted vine, decorated with coloured strings. Women can only watch; they aren't allowed to participate as they are considered impure.

"Even if one menstruating woman attends the zatra, the men will burn their feet," Aajji explains to Carlos. "No matter how much their devotion."

Tara cranes her neck out of the car window and shouts at the dancing men in konkani, "All the best! Mind your feet!" Carlos looks questioningly. She winks at him.

"Blasphemy," he whispers, not wanting Aajji to hear. His catholic conscience is extremely disturbed.

"Let's see if that theory holds water – fire, actually," she whispers back.

The bonfire dies out at 4 a.m. Crowds of onlookers wait in anticipation for the main event. The chanting reaches a crescendo as devotees ready themselves to walk on red-hot coals. The first devotee successfully negotiates the coals. Running towards a banyan tree, he throws his stick at its roots and goes home. This scenario is repeated until the last devotee has done the coal run. Aajji, Carlos and Tara are tired too, from being on their feet all night. As they walk towards the parking lot, Aajji and Carlos continue chattering.

"You know, Carlos, my son had brought his Portuguese friends here, and challenged them to walk on coals."

"Really? Did they do it?"

"The poor *paakhle*[20] burnt their feet!" Aajji giggles like a schoolgirl. "I spent the whole night applying *haldi* paste to their feet. Such soft, smooth soles they had, like a baby's bum! Such terrible blisters they suffered."

---

20. white man, foreigner (Konkani)

"Dad would never do such a thing, he wouldn't have the guts."

"What do you know of your father's guts?" Aajji snaps at Tara. "Ramesh was the only local boy in a football team filled with paakhle," Aajji tells Carlos. "My son was brilliant; the Portuguese couldn't believe a native could excel at their game."

"Don't lie, Aajji. Dad has a limp, how could he play football?"

"You think he was born with it? It was your mother's gift to him," Aajji snaps viciously.

Tara is embarrassed. Couldn't Aajji wait till they got home? Why fight in front of Carlos?

"Don't be mean Aajji, everything can't be mom's fault."

"*It is*, Tara! Your mother drove her fancy car all over my son's leg. That's how he got the limp. He married her and we all know what happened next. Anyway, now he only watches football."

"I had no idea! Dad never told me, Aajji. How come he never talks of his football days?"

"He had to give up the game so early, that's why he doesn't talk."

"Aajji, I play football too, but I dare not walk on those coals," says Carlos, trying to diffuse the tension in the car. "Those Dhonds are really crazy men!"

Tara has avoided the family temple in Ponda for many years. She does not believe in organised religion, nor does she have the time. Besides, when she sent the temple committee a proposal for dredging the bathing tanks in the complex, they asked her for a kickback. Imagine temple trustees and head priests wanting kickbacks.

But Dad and Aajji visit every month, to conduct poojas for her safety and well-being. This year, since she's on leave, Aajji is adamant that she should sit in for a pooja. The dice seems loaded against her, as Dad also joins in the chorus.

"Tara, you are just sitting at home, please go. At least show your face at the family temple, once in a blue moon. That way the community knows you exist."

"Are you two plotting some match-making nonsense? Is there some community function today, that you want me to go and 'show' my face?"

"Nothing like that. The family priest will be happy to see you. So many times he has included your name in the temple newsletter. Go meet him and take his blessings," her dad insists.

Tara had visited their family temple last when she was in school. It was on the occasion of Shigmo festivities her family had hosted. The priests had burnt enough sandalwood and incense to smoke out a forest of beehives. In fact, they must have appeared like one to a fly sitting on the ceiling, their heads bobbing back and forth to prayers, a constant drone emanating from everyone, women in yellow silk saris, covered head to toe in gold jewellery.

The blazing March sun had turned the temple roof into a hot *tava*. Fat lizards scampered over wooden rafters supporting Mangalore roof tiles. Every now and then, a lizard would stray onto a hot tile, scorch its grip, and fall on someone standing below, usually a lady. Resulting in glass-shattering shrieks. The heat and suffering in the name of religion was made bearable by the little tandav that ensued.

When a young priest had announced lunch, there was a stampede. Everyone ran to reserve a spot on mats spread on the floor. Women and men sat in separate rows. The food, served on a banana leaf, was basic *satvik* fare. It tasted divine. Probably, because they were lunching at 5 p.m.

The priests serving food from steel buckets were extremely generous with portions. Tara had watched helplessly as a huge gob of rice landed smack in the middle of her banana leaf. Being seven years old, she didn't know it was okay to waste food, so stoically she finished it all. Also ten puris, three helpings of a vegetable curry and two *vaatis*[21] of sweet kheer, only to puke it all over the banana leaf!

---

21. Small steel bowls

The priests arrive from their nearby quarters, a middle-aged man followed by his young assistant. Tara offers a handshake, but quickly retrieves it as Aajji's bony elbow digs a hole in her ribcage. She does a *namaste*. Aajji introduces her. The head priest smiles recollecting the two-decade-old incident. He is the same priest who had served her copious quantities of food.

"Taraa… the girl who doesn't know when to stop," he says, smiling at her. The young assistant lifts his gaze and looks surreptitiously at her. She catches him.

"How many dead bodies?"

"Pardon?"

"Tell him how many dead bodies you handled on the burning ship," Aajji whispers. Tara is impressed by his interest in her work. "Thirty," she says, "terrible disaster. They've enforced stricter maritime rules for carrying inflammable cargo…"

"You *touched* the dead bodies?"

"How else to get them out? I was wearing gloves." Tara is used to people being either disgusted by her profession or afraid for her safety. She always tries to dispel any fears or doubts. "Bodies were torn apart by the explosion. I lost count of disjointed limbs."

"They weren't whole?" the head priest looks disturbed.

"Most of them weren't."

"My task will be harder," he says to Aajji. The priest and his assistant go inside to discuss something.

Tara whispers to Aajji, "Tell him to do the blessing, why is he chit-chatting about my work?"

"Have patience, Tara."

The priests return. The head priest says to Aajji, "It will cost more-Rs 2500 per spirit."

"Don't worry, I'm carrying extra. Just take them all out," says Aajji, as if discussing with a vet the removal of ticks or maggots from a pet dog.

Tara interrupts. "What money, what spirits? What's going on?"

"Haven't you told her?" the priest asks Aajji.

"She wouldn't have come if I had," Aajji mumbles. "Just do it."

"Excuse me," Tara follows the head priest, "what has my Aajji asked you to do?"

"Exorcism."

"Exorcism!" Tara is aghast. "Aajji you said he'll do a simple birthday blessing!"

"Tara, don't be scared."

"I'm not scared. I'm angry! What a cheap trick, Aajji. I'm going home. Come on your own if you want." Tara starts to walk.

"Tara, please," Aajji runs after her, "it's for your own good."

"Mrs Salgaonkar, if you don't do the exorcism, you'll still have to pay," says the head priest. "We've purchased all articles required for it."

"How much?" Tara asks the head priest.

"2000 rupees, and an extra 500 for cancelling,"

That gives Tara an idea. Walking towards the three conspirators, she calculates the amount Aajji will have to pay, having mentioned thirty bodies.

But most of them were torsos or waist downwards. Half rate for exorcising half spirits – that seems like a fair deal to strike.

"Only five bodies were intact, the rest were just parts. I want a discount," Tara says to the priest.

"Disjointed spirits scatter inside the body, they're more difficult to coax out," the head priest replies. "But we'll give you a discount."

He takes Tara into the *garbha griha* and asks Aajji to leave. "We'll continue late into the night. She'll rest at the ashram afterwards. Send someone to collect her tomorrow morning," he instructs Aajji.

"I can go on my own."

"You won't be in a state to do that," he admonishes Tara. Aajji hands her an envelope filled with cash and bids goodbye. The assistant helps Aajji to a taxi. He returns after fifteen minutes and the exorcism ritual starts.

Two massive brass lamps standing beside the deity are lit up. Rows of lighted wicks flicker, illuminating the dark room, revealing for the first time her family deity's face. Carved from black granite, his broad forehead is smeared with vermilion, sandalwood and turmeric. Large fish-shaped silver eyes stare at her like predators at night. Brass temple bells above her head begin tolling on their own. The chamber fills with a thick, pungent smoke.

"Do you see bad dreams?" The head priest thunders.

"Nightmares, you mean?"

"Same thing, what do you see?"

"I see ghosts," she says, remembering a Bruce Willis movie. "They stop me on the road and talk to me."

"What do they tell you?" the priest asks.

"They tell me I should walk around naked."

The hand held brass bells suddenly ring with less gusto. Smearing vermilion powder on her forehead, the head priest mumbles some mantras. He starts patting her with a small *jhaadoo*. Tara starts giggling.

"See how they mock me," he says to his assistant. Looking at Tara he says, "Go away, return where you came from."

Tara turns around and starts walking to the exit.

"Not you, I'm telling the spirits." He calls out to her, "Come back, don't leave halfway; your life is in danger."

"Stop it! I don't believe this nonsense…" Tara shouts.

"Then why agree to it? You could've gone home with your Aajji. Don't waste our time," he says angrily.

"I've recorded everything with my mobile. I'm going to expose you. I'll also stop by the Income Tax Office. All that cash with no bills or receipts… how many people do you swindle in a day?"

The head priest suddenly changes his tune. "Listen child, if you don't believe, it won't work. Lots of people benefit from our service. We don't want your money," he says, returning it. "No exorcism, no money."

Tara leaves the temple. She has absolutely no intention of returning the money to Aajji.

21

Kapiyaalis

Aajji is sitting on the floor, hunched over her *kapiyaalis*[22]. "Back so soon? You were supposed to return tomorrow?" she asks, surprised to see Tara.

"Those dead sailors came out faster than expected."

"Wait!" Aajji asks her to stay put on the threshold. She rushes to the kitchen and returns with something in hand. Tara rolls her eyes. "You're removing my *dixtt*[23] now? No more purification required; it's all taken care of."

"Extra caution never hurt anybody," Aajji says, circling a closed fist clockwise and anti clockwise over Tara's head, then chucking the tiny balls of dough over her shoulders and saying a loud *thoo*. "Touch my feet." Tara does as she is told.

"I'm starving."

"First go wash all that vermilion and turmeric from your forehead," says Aajji. Tara goes to the washbasin. Aajji follows her. "Hope those priests did a good job. So much money they took…"

---

22. Patch work quilt (Konkani)

23. Evil eye (Konkani)

"Oh absolutely," Tara replies, pushing the large chunk of hash bought with the same money, deeper into her pocket. "Took out every spirit. Not one left."

"I'm so relieved."

"Can I eat now?" she asks after a brief pause.

"Bai, go get something from the *posro*[24]. I didn't cook as you were going to stay at the ashram. Dad's at a football match, he'll eat out," Aajji tells her.

"Oh Aajji, I'm so hungry, and now I have to go out and get the food. When is Dad back?"

"Anytime now," says Aajji. "Tara, don't tell him, okay? He thinks we went for a routine birthday blessing. And I told him that afterwards you went to stay at a friend's place. Now make some excuse for not staying at your friend's."

Half an hour later, Tara returns, laden with food parcels, munching on a *bhaji pav*. Aajji is still engrossed in her kapiyaalis.

"What's this new design, Aajji?" Tara enquires, looking at the triangular fabric pieces scattered all around.

"Roopa's getting married by April end. She wants five kapiyaalis for her trousseau."

"Charge her."

"Tara, money's not everything. These are my blessings."

"You're quite generous when blessing other people's kids."

"Let your marriage get fixed, then see how many kapiyaalis I make for you," Aajji says.

"Aajji, I'm afraid you'll have to wait forever."

---

24. Area in a village with shops and food stalls

"*Shee-shee*, don't talk like that… things will change, just wait and see," says Aajji, putting down her kapiyaali. "Your destiny will improve, now that the exorcism is done."

"You think so?" Tara smiles, remembering what happened.

"You did well by coming to the temple and undergoing the exorcism. I was so afraid you'd make a scene, but you kept your Aajji's respect," she continues. "Your life was packed with bad spirits. They're gone now. There's room for good to enter."

Tara imagines walking around with a sticker on her forehead, the words **For Rent** written in bold. "And what's this *good* you talk about?"

"First your marriage will get fixed," Aajji smiles indulgently, "then you can leave your job. Be a good wife and mother."

Tara chokes on her food as she tries to stifle a laugh.

"I'm serious. I've already thought of some great designs for you," Aajji says. "I'll do a sea and underwater theme with boats, fish, sea horses, mermaids, and of course, your starfish."

"On one kapiyaali?"

"You think I'm so stingy? Each on a separate kapiyaali."

"Wow, Aajji! But forget the mermaids, okay?"

"They're beautiful."

"No Aajji, they're ugly and they get me into trouble."

"I'll make beautiful ones, like you've never seen before."

Aajji always has the last word when it comes to kapiyaalis. All the young brides of Saligao have to have at least two of her handmade quilts in their wedding trousseau; they are a good luck charm. Marriages do not last otherwise. Aajji does not mind the burden it puts on her.

Hoarding scraps of cloth in separate bundles marked according to colours, textures and prints, she sits hunched for hours, especially before wedding season. Churning out intricate designs by sheer force of will power, her small dried up frame at loggerheads with the fierce look of determination in her eyes.

Aajji is also a diligent recycler. It's not unusual for Tara to find her old clothes reincarnated as new quilts for some poor unsuspecting soul. Aajji doesn't even spare Tara's discarded underwear, cutting bits and shaping them into flower or bird patches. Even Tara finds it difficult to recognize those bits that had once hugged tight her nether regions. Observing Roopa's collection, Tara wonders how many clothes must have gone missing from her wardrobe this time.

Aajji has seen all the eligible young men and women of Saligao get married. Only Tara remains. Tired of being asked when she'll make kapiyaalis for her own granddaughter, Aajji has stopped attending weddings. She visits the previous day, for the *Roce* or *Haldi* ceremonies and presents the bride with kapiyaalis and blessings.

Every year Aajji relaxes the conditions for Tara's marriage. In college, it was, *Tara should marry by twenty-two, immediately after graduation.*

Tara had nightmares in which she ran to her wedding hall dressed in a graduation gown. Taking it off with flourish, she would show off her wedding sari worn underneath. On really bad nights, she took off the graduation gown and was aghast to find herself naked underneath.

When Tara turned twenty-five, it became, *Forget the horoscope matching, and just get a nice boy from our community.* No luck. Tara turned twenty-eight, inching close to the dreaded thirties. *Non-Goan boys will do, look at Bombay boys too… as long as they are Hindu.*

Tara has turned thirty-two, and Aajji has been making polite enquiries about her diver colleagues. Suddenly Catholic boys will also do, as long as they are *Roman Catholic Brahmins*.

Aajji mutters a new mantra these days. "Time is running out. What will you do Tara; time is running out for you. All the young men will get married and no one will be left for you. You will have to choose a husband from 'Widowers with children' men, 'One leg shorter than the other' men, 'Divorced' men, 'Old enough to be your father' men. Oh god! Time is running out."

Tara rolls a joint and mulls over the eventful day. Aajji has unwittingly sponsored her quota for the month.

22

A Handful of Starfish

One evening, as she is about to enter a café in Candolim, Tara hears someone shout, "Mad mermaid!" She ignores it, being accustomed to all kinds of taunts since the parade. A few seconds later, someone taps her shoulder. Turning around to confront whoever it is, she is relieved to see Balgo.

"Oh, it's you!" Tara says, her heart still pounding.

"How are you? Finished work early today?"

"I'm fine, Balgo. I'm on a three-month vacation," she replies. "My leaves had piled up…"

"That's great! Any travel plans?"

"There's a company guest house at Colva. No *trekking-shekking* for me, maybe Kerala… let's see."

"Outside India? Sri Lanka? Lovely beaches!" Balgo offers suggestions.

"Don't want to spend much… the company guest house is free."

"Colva's a good place. Some hidden islands and coves are perfect for diving."

"So, what's up, Balgo? Any more parties?" Tara asks.

"Just small ones in discos here and there; nothing big, not without you."

"Not without me?"

"I would definitely invite you for something big," he says. "Wish I'd known you were on leave."

"Just few weeks since I started. Two-and-a-half months more to go! Anyway, can't do that party stuff anymore, I'm getting old!"

"If you aren't in a hurry, let's sit and talk?" Balgo asks, pointing to a corner table.

Tara agrees, as she has lots to talk too. About the pond, Bholenath Guruji, the police case. "How's Bholenath Guruji?"

"He remembers you," Balgo replies, and is amused when she blushes. "Why, just the other day he said we should organise a party at the Casa – then we can call you to clean the pond!"

"Really?"

"Just kidding! Visit us Tara, you don't need a party or a pond de-silting."

"I don't make social visits to clients."

"Aaah! Here I am, thinking of you as a friend. After all that we experienced before and after the party – that *really* was some party, wasn't it? A party that ended all parties at the Casa!"

"You mean there won't be any more?"

"Yeah, Bholenath Guruji doesn't want to take another chance. He's already under the scanner because of that one night. What a night!"

"You're telling me!" Tara says. "I'm surprised the dead couple story wasn't in the papers next day. What happened?"

"Some suicide pact. Cops found a note in their hotel room. Luckily no drugs were found in their bodies during autopsy. We paid the newspapers to not report it."

"They were making love in my room before the party started, and next day I see them in the pond."

"Oh, you didn't tell me this," Balgo says to her.

"I was… shocked." Tara replies, a glazed look settling in her eyes as she remembers the incident. Balgo notices it and immediately changes the subject.

"So how come your boss gave you leave? Thought you were indispensible, Tara."

"He thinks I'm overworked and burnt out. And there's some other stuff. He's hiring a navy diver to be *my* boss. I've been sent on leave while the naval guy transitions into his new civilian role. Bloody office politics, I tell you."

"Problem with working in an office is you *cannot* avoid the politics. The solution is – don't work at all! So glad I'm done with work."

She laughs. "Balgo, *you*, in an office?"

"I was different in an earlier life."

"You mean, you've worn ties and stuff?"

"Suspenders even."

"Investment banker?" She's curious.

"Not that bad. Sound engineer with an Australian music company, late nineties. Got tired of packaging boy bands, so I quit."

"Then?"

I went back to University of Canberra to study indigenous music. Did my thesis on Aboriginal Music. You see, I'm half Aborigine from my mother's side."

So that's the accent!

"I studied various instruments, their pitches… and began dabbling in the ritual and spiritual side of music, its use in narration of dreamtime stories.."

"Stories about dreams? I could tell a new one every day!"

"Not the dreams you and I see; dreams my aboriginal ancestors saw millennia ago. Visions that explained how life in the universe evolved—" he stops. "Am I blabbering?"

"No, go on!" Tara says to him.

"I met Bholenath Guruji at one of his parties; we got talking about my culture, my music, my didgeridoo. He invited me to join as sound engineer. And I worked on the frequencies to induce better trance states."

"Interesting," says Tara. "I thought drugs induced a trance."

"BPMs of 150 and above push listeners to a heightened level of awareness – the state of trance. Lighting and drugs add to it – like icing on a cake, but music's the base of trance – the cake so to speak."

"And you've done like serious research on… baking?"

"Haha, sort of…"

A quick glance at her watch reveals it is dinner time. Her folks have become used to seeing her home by 7.30 – latest by 8 p.m. these past few weeks.

"You're on holiday!" Balgo protests. "I was about to ask you to join me. I'm going to the night market. My friends are performing tonight."

"Next Saturday perhaps."

They ride out together on their respective scooters. Balgo has an ancient Bajaj, it sputters and spits, trying to keep pace with Tara's manic Kinetic. She waits at the Saligao crossroad to bid him goodbye. Arpora and the Saturday Night Market are a couple of kilometres from here.

"I'll see you to your house, the roads are quite deserted," Balgo insists and follows her.

She takes a narrow road snaking through a tightly-knit village. A kilometre inside, they are in a thick wooded forest. She stops at the entrance of her orchard and opens the iron gate, "Thanks for accompanying me."

"You live in this forest?"

"It's a mango and jackfruit orchard." She laughs. "My folks live in the big house we just passed. I live in the guest house."

"Won't you invite me in?"

"It's late," she says sheepishly. "Come again during daytime. Get your latest psy-trance mixes..."

She closes the gate and walks inside. There's no sound of his scooter being kick-started. Turning around to see what the matter is, she sees Balgo opening her gate and running frantically towards her.

"Tara! I need to use your toilet, loosies!"

"Oh! Come in quick." She hurriedly opens the door and directs him to the guest toilet. In the meantime, she rifles through her medicine cabinet. Five minutes later, Balgo steps out looking pale but relieved. "Take this tablet. It'll help." She hands him a glass of water.

"Thank you. Had chicken xec xec for lunch. Was tasty, but... Let me sit for 5 minutes, okay?"

"So many fish tanks," he says, looking around. "How do you look after them?"

"Oh, these are the smaller ones... got bigger ones in my bedroom. Not so difficult really."

"We have one at the Casa, basic two-and-half feet by one foot, and we fight over who'll clean it," says Balgo, going closer to inspect. "Why only starfish, don't you like other fish?"

"Everybody keeps gold fish, guramis and other fresh water fish. I prefer marine fish. I've collected these starfish during my deep sea dives."

"Nice! You know, I've only seen small spiny ones at Baga," he says, kneeling down for a better view. "These are so colourful. Look at that, it's like two feet long! Wow Tara, this is a serious hobby. It's beyond hobby; it's an obsession… but not in a bad way."

"Ya, been obsessed since I was five. Went for my first sea swim and stepped out of the waves with a starfish entangled in my hair!"

"So the starfish chose you," says Balgo, mesmerised by her fish tanks. Tara gets a little concerned as he transfers fingerprints and impressions of his oily face on the aquarium glass. She gently pulls him away.

"When I was little, I reached for the stars. And got a handful of starfish."

"Poem?" he asks.

"My personal quote. See, I wasn't aiming for stars in the sky, I was chasing their reflection."

"I should go now," he says. "Free tomorrow?"

"It's Sunday, I'm cleaning my tanks."

"Spare an hour, I want to gift you something you've always wanted."

"Don't remember asking for anything."

"Tara, have you erased the entire party from your memory? You *did* ask for something. You'll get it tomorrow!"

23

Tara Gets Inked

"Hey! Are you taking me to Calangute beach? I hate it, reminds me of Juhu."

"*Joo who?* Patience, Tara!"

Balgo's Bajaj coughs and farts along the straight beach road, lined on both sides with trinket shops and beachwear stalls. Racks of brightly-coloured clothes flutter in the late afternoon breeze. Batik shawls, tie & dye t-shirts and sarongs in vivid colours compete with each other to captivate passersby.

Psychedelic, hot and fluorescent, the stalls light up the drug trail leading to the beaches, like lights on a runway. Beacons directing you towards lift off, and subsequently, touchdowns. Sometimes, even crash landings.

He swerves off the narrow tar road, taking a dirt track heading towards Anjuna village. On reaching the left going downhill to the beach, he manoeuvres sharply from the road, into a hamlet beside. Tara shuffles uneasily on her pillion seat; she doesn't ride this way.

A considerable distance from the main road, this is where some hippies have settled. Living in ramshackle peasant houses, bought dirt-cheap. Their original inhabitants have moved into pokey apartments elsewhere. A hippie ghetto, where anyone who is not, feels distinctly out of place.

Domestic tourists from Karnataka and hinterland Maharashtra drive their Mahindra Trax jeeps aimlessly, looking for cheap thrills. Some hippie women have resorted to prostitution, to feed drug dependencies that have dented their finances and their bodies. Tourists come seeking this dazed, emaciated white flesh.

Parking his Bajaj on a street facing a crumbling villa, Balgo casually remarks, "Bet you didn't expect this, Tara," and points to Fred's Tattoo Parlour.

"You're getting another tattoo on your bum, and you want me to watch? Don't remember asking for that, Balgo."

He laughs, pushing her inside a graffiti-splattered doorway. Once inside, Tara is enthralled. She strolls as if in an art gallery, studying the sample designs pasted on the walls. All the usual suspects are in abundance: skulls, butterflies, broken hearts, arrow-pierced bleeding hearts, and big-breasted naked women.

She scrutinises a Jim Morrison tattoo, stopping a while to appreciate Marilyn Monroe in her famous skirt billowing pose. Skipping a section filled with psychedelic trance imagery, she walks towards a wall displaying designs of Hindu gods and goddesses. Pointing to Saraswati and Lakshmi, she laughs, "Who'd want that pair?"

"They're selling like hot cakes," says a deadpan male voice

Tara turns to see a wizened old hippie. His silver grey hair is braided, reaching to his waist, where it peters to a rat's tail. Wrinkles crisscross his face; his large forehead has an Om symbol tattooed prominently in its centre. Wearing a Ganesha t-shirt under a black leather jacket, he stands with his tattoo machine held gun-like, James Bond style.

"Tara, meet Fred, he owns this parlour," Balgo says, walking over and giving him a hug.

"Why don't you like those goddess tattoos?" Fred asks her, as they shake hands.

"I'm an atheist," she replies.

"Cool, there are other designs you can choose."

Balgo interrupts, "Here's the design," he shows Fred an intricate drawing of a starfish done in the aboriginal style.

"Beautiful! And where do you want this one?"

"Oh, not on me," says Balgo, pushing Tara forward, "On her."

"No ways!" Tara squeaks, the blood draining from her face.

"You've always wanted a tattoo, that's what you said. So when I saw your starfish last night, I got an idea. Went home and quickly sketched this for you."

"*Arrey*! When did I ever say I want a tattoo?"

"Decide fast," Fred says gruffly, "or I'll take another customer."

"Please take another customer," Tara tells Fred.

Balgo thinks she's afraid of contracting HIV or Hepatitis. "Fred has a certificate from the, umm, International Association of Tattoo Artists… for adhering to the strictest safety regulations. Don't you, Fred?" Fred looks at him cross-eyed. Tara sees it.

"Miss, I sterilise all my equipment," Fred says to her. "Get new sets every three months, and I only use disposable needles. I have a stable hand, give me any design and I can copy it." Fred points to a familiar design on the wall. "I've tattooed that on Balgo." Turning to Balgo he says, "Show her."

"I've seen it."

"Tara, don't worry about the pain. There are parts of the body where it doesn't hurt much," Balgo pacifies her.

Lying face down on Fred's couch, jeans lowered to where her buttocks begin, she whimpers. With every prick of the needle (there are lots, Balgo has made a small but intricate design), she moans and sighs, hurling the choicest abuses at both men. At one point, she turns her head and finds Balgo staring intently at her butt crack. But Fred is all concentration.

She wonders if tattoo artists ever get turned on whilst tattooing people on different body parts. Perhaps they are like doctors; they distance themselves from their subjects. And they have to be extremely patient too.

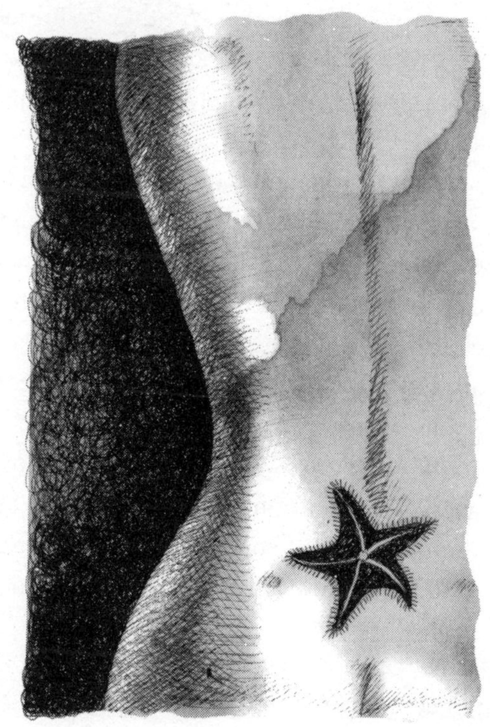

Fred stops when Tara begs him, continues only when she says yes; taking an hour to render a tattoo that would normally take twenty minutes. Minor finishing touches done, he pastes a cling film on the tattooed area, to prevent blood from oozing onto her clothes. She bolts, not wanting to spend an extra second inside the parlour, and sits on Balgo's scooter parked on the road.

Tara cribs throughout the ride. "Like it or not?" Balgo snaps at her, turning off the ignition. They are at the gate of her house. Tara dismounts. "There's enough pain at work. Now this…"

"It'll go away tomorrow."

"This is my first and last tattoo."

"Said all the people who then got addicted! Not a millimetre to spare on their bodies, yet they go for more…"

"Ya, I've seen those freaks. Pretty sure I won't be like them!"

"Agreed… but, one or two more and you'll still be within limits."

"No thanks," she says and starts walking away.

Balgo puts his Bajaj on the side stand and runs to catch up with her. She avoids looking at him. Facing her, he starts pulling out her tucked-in shirt. Tara angrily pushes him away. He comes closer and slides his palms inside her jeans, massaging her back around the tattoo in a slow, circular motion. She resists, both palms wedged firmly between his chest and hers, but the pain starts ebbing slowly and she relaxes into his embrace. He is about to kiss her but stops as she closes her eyes in anticipation. "Someone called your name; I think it's your grandmother."

"Run," Tara whispers, quickly tucking in her shirt.

24

Sea of Pain

Another tormenting night stretches ahead of Tara. The nagging pain caused by her tattoo bothers her. Trying not to focus on it, she wishes Balgo had stayed a bit longer to massage it away. Whatever he did for those few seconds seemed to work. She wonders if he's sitting on a beach somewhere, laughing at the stars. He has no idea how high her pain threshold is, she can bear all kinds of pain but she has needle phobia.

Divers need to be inoculated regularly against infection and disease. It's a long-standing joke among her colleagues; they love seeing Tara humbled by a small syringe.

It is her family doctor's fault, the one they consulted when she was a child. He belonged to the old school of medicine, mixing his potions, making his own pills. He did not prescribe antibiotics, unless the patient was dying. He did not give injections.

Tara got used to his gentle medicine. Her childhood coincided with the AIDS epidemic in India, with the first case reported in Goa due to infected needles. Tara grew up fearing injections.

But everything else she can take. Like that one afternoon after finishing an assignment…

Taking off her flippers, she walked barefoot on a deserted shore, relishing the feel of warm sand. All of a sudden, a piercing pain radiated through her right foot. Looking down she saw a rusted iron sheet, buried edge upwards in sand. It had neatly sliced the little toe off her right foot. Blood flowed copiously, forming a red halo around her foot. Steadying herself, she looked for the separated toe amongst sea shells and pebbles. Found the forlorn digit and held it in her palm. Severed from her foot, it could be admired from angles not seen before. Tara chucked it into the sea – it was useless. Fish food.

The chief surgeon at the Bambolim GMC hospital was livid. Couldn't she have packed it in ice and brought it along? They would have stitched it back with microsurgery. The interns would have benefited from the practice. After dressing her foot, he pulled out a syringe. And Tara bawled like a child.

For months later she had sudden inexplicable urges to scratch her non-existent toe. A truant mind tricked her into believing it was still attached to her body. Fingers reaching absent-mindedly met an empty space where the little digit once sat, beside four others.

The memory of pain is as real as the pain. It persists.

Tara can still feel Fred's needle at work. Like a horde of tiny black ants have gnawed under her skin, arranged themselves in a starfish pattern, biting continuously even as they settle.

Standing before her full-length bedroom mirror, she observes the tattoo once more. A bit difficult to get a full view; twisting and turning her torso into awkward positions, she manages to see a small portion. On completing it, Fred had positioned her between two mirrors placed at an angle, giving her a full view of her back. In the dim light of his parlour, she saw for the first time how her back appeared to others: a few spinal cord digits jutting out and two dimples above her buttocks. Just her luck, to have a pair of dimples on her butt.

The black ants bite less viciously as Tara strokes them to sleep. Her hands rest in front of her, but the tattoo continues being massaged. *Who is massaging her?*

Perplexed, she turns to look and feels the coolness of water.

Afloat in liquid mercury, everywhere she looks a million Taras look back at her. A little further, she spots seaweed of red, blue and green colours. Fish with fluorescent scales swim languidly in between. She waits in anticipation for something to show up, not sure what it will be. Finally they arrive, swimming in her direction, a school of starfish in varying sizes, all of them translucent, their body fluids visible as they glide gracefully above. She wants to catch some for her fish tank. Not having seen translucent starfish before, she has no idea they existed. Swimming towards a beautiful one, she extends her arm to trap it. Suddenly, the ocean turns hostile, the water – thick and viscous.

The long stalks of seaweed that were caressing her just seconds ago, start entwining around her body. But she's not afraid; she surrenders, allowing herself to be trapped. Just as quickly, they turn into blond dreadlocks. Standing suspended in water, she is held firmly by them. The starfish swim teasingly close. Getting bolder they settle all over her body. The moment they come in contact with her skin, they melt and seep inside. Leaving so many starfish tattoos all over.

Tara sits upright on her bed. What will Aajji say when she sees all the tattoos – *damn, it was just a dream! What a relief!*

She's shivering, having kicked away her bed sheet. Leaning forward to pull it back, she is stunned to see her naked body. Her t-shirt and pyjamas are on the floor. Tara distinctly remembers going to bed fully clothed. Her bed sheet is soaked and so is the rest of her body. Even her hair is dripping wet. She squeezes water out and looks for a towel. A chill runs down her spine as her fingers encounter a baby starfish stuck in her hair. Rushing to return it to its tank, she finds the tank cover open.

Now this is strange. Did she forget to close it after feeding them? Of course not, she closed it tight.

25

Sailors who Hate Tattoos

Carlos calls Tara routinely during lunch time since she started her leave. To update her on what's happening at Martins'. He's anxious today because Gregory was in office.

"*Bai*, he asked us all how we got along with you. Trick questions. Were you a good boss? Did we like working under you? So on and so forth."

"What did you say?" Tara asked.

"I said you trained me well, coached me for the license exam. Don't know about others… should I find out?"

"Nah, it's okay, Carlos."

"He's meeting you later."

"You mean I have to come to work for *this*?"

"No, he'll visit you at home," Carlos informs her.

Tara has to cancel her date with Balgo. There's no way to get in touch; he doesn't own a cellphone. She'll call the Casa landline, leave a message, and pray he gets it before setting out. Unlikely though. He'll come to the café, unaware of the change in her plans. After an hour of waiting, he'll go elsewhere.

Gregory shows up at 4 p.m., dressed casually in faded jeans and a collarless maroon t-shirt, not tucked inside. Looking like a civilian, except for his still severe crew cut. He holds a package that he is very conscious of. Putting it down, picking it up, looking around for some other place to keep it, and picking it up again.

"Should I call the bomb squad?" Tara asks.

He avoids her gaze. "Just some saris. One for you and one for your Aajji. So many sari shops in Cochin. Whenever I return from a posting, I get saris for friends and family."

"Bribing me?"

Gregory laughs.

Tara always worries when guys drop hints like that. Gifts of saris, bangles and other dainty women thingies can mean only one thing – they are laying a trap. To wrap you and trap you in five yards of fabric. And concurrently bind your hands with tiny glass bangles, toes with silver rings.

But you look so graceful in a sari, so beautiful. And, the woman falls for it, flattered with the attention. Falling hard. Falling in line.

Not her. She's no performing monkey.

Just then Gregory receives a call on his mobile. He breaks into a wide smile. "Right now?" he asks. "Okay, I'll leave." Looking at Tara, he says, "My cousin sister just delivered a baby boy. Sorry, I'll have to leave right away. Tara, can I ask you a small favour? I want to discuss some problematic issues at work."

She wonders if he's quitting in just a few weeks of joining. After all, commercial diving is not a naval divers' chai glass. "Sure, how can I help?"

"Come with me – if you aren't doing anything – we'll discuss on the way," Gregory tells her.

"To the hospital?"

"No, home."

"Can't it wait till tomorrow?"

"Mr Martin wants my report tonight. I'm making a presentation on improving safety standards at Martins' Dredging," says Gregory.

"Ha, good luck with that!" She laughs. And wonders why he is making PowerPoint presentations instead of diving.

"Please come, my folks want to meet the girl who stopped a Carnaval!"

"Will I ever be able to get rid of that tag? Bloody hell! It was all your fault. I'm going to tell your folks, wait!"

"They *know*. I mean, my mom has scolded and lectured me enough."

⚓

Gregory lives in Chorao, an island on the Mandovi River, and a classified bird sanctuary. They reach Ribandar at 6 p.m. just as the office crowd readies to go home. Ferries carry cars, bikes, and small tempos, along with people, across the river. Nothing fancy, they are just noisy diesel guzzlers that pollute rivers.

Gregory and Tara sit on his parked Enfield as there is no standing space. Car owners sit inside their cars, while other commuters sit on top of bonnets and dickeys. Within minutes, the ferry docks at Chorao jetty, surrounded on three sides by thick mangroves. All engines come alive, frightening the jetty mudskippers into burrowing deeper in the sticky sand. Gregory's the first to zoom off; it's his terrain.

He takes a narrow road slicing through a thick cover of trees. Gulmohars and Amaltas are in full bloom all around. In less than a month, rains will arrive, stripping them of their blanket of flowers and transferring it on the forest floor. An undulating river snakes through the island, branching into smaller rivulets as it reaches the interior. Kingfishers flash brilliant colours, skimming the water surface for fish in the last light of the day. Storks, herons, cormorants, and egrets return to roost in the trees. Squawking incessantly, they create quite a racket. Bird sanctuaries must be the noisiest places on earth to live in. As they reach the island interior, the forest cover thins into clearings with small fields and houses. Gregory takes an elevated mud road that goes through a dried up paddy field. At its far end is his house.

Goan houses never cease to amaze Tara. Especially their exterior colour schemes; combinations that will make any big-city architect blush. This one is baby pink with white trimmings. Windows and doors are painted a rich cobalt blue. The compound wall is freshly white washed and hugged by a profusion of bougainvillea. Anywhere else in the country, it would have looked disastrous, like an oversize dollhouse. But in Chorao, with its colourful forest cover, and the river song close by, it looks perfect.

Gregory's entire family – his parents, a twin pair of old spinster aunts from his father's side, come out to greet Tara.

"So you are the famous Tara," his mother says with a twinkle in her eye, as she comes forward to hug and kiss her.

"Infamous is more like it. How are you Mrs Figuerido?."

After she get hugs and kisses from the old aunts and Gregory's dad, his mom says, "My dear, you are very brave. It was my Gregory's fault, I'm apologising for him. I'm so happy to finally meet you, Tara. You are always welcome at our home. But today we have to go to Margao. My niece, Rita, has delivered a baby boy. Rita's like my daughter, grew up in this house… Please stay for dinner. Sorry we can't be good hosts today."

"Gregory, why don't you go too? I'll come back some other time."

"No, he'll stay. Someone has to be home always, my sisters-in-law have Alzheimer's," Mrs Figueiredo says, pointing to the bent ladies, "they have to be watched at all times."

His parents bid goodbye and leave.

The sala is large enough to be a mini dance hall. With Spanish floor tiles and antique furniture of dark teak wood, it looks like a museum exhibit of a typical turn of the century Goan villa. Easy chairs with wirework in lattice designs have armrests that open out into leg-rests – relics from the past, now seen mostly in wayside antique shops. Chandeliers of green and blue glass adorn the ceiling. The walls are covered with framed photographs. Tara looks at each one, as Gregory goes to the kitchen to fetch wine.

"So handsome you look here, how old were you in this picture?" she calls out.

"Not me! Marcus, my older brother."

"Older? You could be twins!"

"Sixteen years between us. Looked just like me when he was young."

"How old is he here?"

"Eighteen… Just before he ran off to Portugal, with Aunt Clara."

"Aunt Clara?"

"Mom's younger sister. Aunt Clara is my cousin Rita's mother," he says, giving Tara a wine glass.

"Wait, your eighteen-year-old brother ran away with his own married aunt? *Arrey wah! Hero murey!*" Tara squeals. "How old was she?"

"Twenty-four-year-old mother with a two-year-old child she conveniently left behind."

"C'mon, she was in love! What about her husband, your uncle?"

"Uncle Miguel drank himself to death."

"Oh the collateral damage of love. Are Marcus and Clara still together?"

"Don't know; we've cut relations."

Tara points her wine glass to the photograph and raises a toast, "To illicit liaisons."

"To happy marriages," he corrects.

"To Marcus and Clara."

"To women who'll one day wear saris." He smiles, pointing his glass to her.

"Never!"

"C'mon, it's got a Lycra halter blouse with brocade work. *Palav* and borders also have the same brocade work."

"You wear no, if you like it so much!"

"Tara please… just for me? Show me na how you look in it. Please?"

"No ways! But I want to see the blouse. If it's a good pattern, I'll get a similar one stitched."

"Why stitch a new one, keep this. Sari I'll give to Rita; the blouse won't fit her." Gregory says, handing her the packet. Tara opens it and holds the blouse against her torso.

"Wear it and see."

Taking off her t-shirt, she wears the blouse. Gregory takes her to his parent's bedroom. It has an old-fashioned full-length mirror with three sections. The bike ride has messed her hair; it sits on her shoulders like a dry mop. Holding it up, he helps her knot the blouse at the nape of her neck. It's a perfect fit.

"Nice?" she asks him.

"No."

"No?" she checks her reflection again.

"A sari blouse looks nice on a sari, not with jeans. You look like those hippie freaks, mixing and matching clothes that don't belong together."

Tara is bewildered by his choice of words. He could've just said *she* doesn't look good.

"Wear the sari and see how beautiful they look together."

Snatching the sari from him, she throws just the palav over her shoulder.

"Oi! Allow me," he says, taking it from her. "I used to help mom drape her saris."

Holding on to one end of the sari, he circles her. She's about to protest, but decides to watch the fun instead. He pushes the top portion inside her jeans, hands straying a lot deeper than required; she smiles.

Stepping on the pile of silk spread on the floor, he apologises and trips, undoing the entire sari. Starting all over, only this time, he manages to wrap himself in it too. Tara starts to giggle. Pleating the palav, he pins it to her blouse, and the pleats at her waist come undone. Putting his hands up, he pretends to be exasperated, but it's obvious he's enjoying it.

"Mom was a teacher at my school. She would always be late in the morning, with the cooking, cleaning and all the housework she had to complete before leaving home. So I would help her with the sari. She's retired now, she can take all the time in the world to wear one," he says sheepishly. "And as you can see, I'm out of practice."

Tara smiles. *Mama's boy*.

Shoving the pleats back into her jeans, he evens out the creases at the small of her back and stops. "There's a bruise here, Tara. Wait, not a bruise, it looks like…,"

"A tattoo. See, it's a starfish," she says, pulling down her jeans just a bit.

"Where'd you get it? Flea market?"

"Maybe. It's beautiful, no?"

"Are you out of your mind? Better get checked for god knows how many diseases. The style's unusual. Who did it?"

"My friend designed it, and his friend tattooed it."

"Girls from good families don't get tattoos. Does Aajji know? And dad?"

Tara bursts out laughing. "I knew you'd say something like that."

"They don't know. I see! What next? Roaming naked on streets so people can see it?"

"Just a tattoo! Most beauty parlours do it, so bloody common!"

"Which beauty parlour you got *yours* from?"

"Not from a parlour... "

"Then?"

"Forget it! I'm leaving. You and your bloody lectures..."

"I'm concerned about your safety, Tara. I would've taken you, to the best tattoo parlour in Goa. You never showed interest before, not even in my tattoos," he complains. "I would've taken you..."

"Didn't want *you* to take me."

"Fine, just pray you're safe." Gregory yanks out the sari from her body, makes a ball and flings it to a corner.

26

Meetings with a Diver in Exile

Balgo reads *The Goan*, seated in his favourite corner at Café Anjuna, while he waits for Tara to arrive. They've been meeting regularly for close to a month now, ever since they bumped into each other at Candolim. She's become his daily fix; he suffers withdrawal symptoms if he doesn't see her for two days.

Why, just yesterday he waited till midnight, worried as hell if she was okay. Unlike most Goans, Tara is a stickler for punctuality, so he knew she wasn't coming at all when she didn't arrive within five minutes of their appointed time. Dejected, he almost called her from the café landline.

In their first few meetings– he hates to call them dates– they were like buddies chatting over coffee. Teasing, laughing hysterically, punching each other's arms. But lately the façade has fallen; their conversations have become more intimate. He catches himself speaking softly, barely audible for her to hear. Tara has to lean closer to take in every word he says. She has a strange habit; she takes off her shoes and places her bare feet on his, whenever they sit across each other at a café.

The first time she did it, she casually remarked that her feet were always cold, and if he didn't mind, could she warm them on his? Sheepishly explaining that her frequent diving caused confusion in her body's thermostat; her extremities were always cold, even in the midst of summer. Readily taking off his floaters, he became her personal foot warmer.

He wonders how they look together. *Are they beginning to look like lovers?* A sure indicator of the change in their status is that the waiters leave them alone. Nowadays they sit undisturbed and unattended, till they signal for something. And even that takes its own sweet time coming.

This has been going on for a while – a month is a while, isn't it? They always find something to talk about. She doesn't talk much, but whatever she says, he finds fascinating. *Is it infatuation? If it is, it's not deep*. He can snap out of it whenever he wants, just like that. He snaps his finger and turns over to the sports page of the newspaper.

Just then, Tara walks into the cafe and pulls a chair opposite him. "Sorry about yesterday, Balgo. Had a briefing with the new boss."

"It's okay, I didn't wait, had things to do," he lies.

Tara, her name is her destiny. Shining above his horizon, she grows brighter by the day. Try as he might, he cannot peel his eyes away. Don't stars shine brightest when they're about to die? Moments before they explode they emit an unnatural glow. This one's going to scorch him for certain when she goes. He's standing too close.

"Packed for Colva? Leaving tomorrow, right?"

"Not yet, don't know where to start," Tara says.

"You'll be on the beach, won't need much!"

"I'm dreading it. I'll die of boredom."

"Tara, be okay with boredom. You don't have to work all the time. You know, this break has done you good."

"Really?"

"Yeah. When I first met you, you had a haunted look in your eyes. That's gone. You look happier now, healthier in fact."

She laughs. "I'm sleeping a lot. But, it'll be back. All I need is one more Andalusia… and *tantadaan!*"

"Tara, I've always wanted to ask you this…" he says hesitantly, "I'd imagine a Hindu Goan girl like you to be traditional and religious. But you aren't…"

"I'm *very* religious! I worship work. But yeah, I'm not traditional. That's coz I'm a Bombay girl at heart." She laughs. "My parents are to blame, especially mom. Also a Bombay girl. Dad visits the temple once a month, mostly to keep Aajji happy. Doubt if he believes though, it's more of a social visit. You could call my parents borderline atheists. And, there's my job…"

"How's your job responsible?" he asks.

"Well, how do I say this…" she stares at her hands, then

looks up. "You know, Balgo, death comes randomly. I've seen it during search ops. There's no pattern, no big plan in the universe. We come, we go. Dust to dust, water to water. Difficult to accept. This randomness of life and death... we need a reason to stay alive, if we know we're going to die anyway! I think that's why we created god. So we can dump all our problems on him. Convenient, right? No need to take responsibilities for the fucked up things we do, no?"

"Hmmm." He wonders who has hurt her so bad. "So you take full responsibility for all the fucked up things you do."

"I try."

The evening seems rather reluctant to pass into night. Suspended over the horizon a few minutes longer than usual, the sun is afraid to dive into the ocean. They wait for it, watching the end-of-season tourists frolicking on the beach.

Summer will soon be over and the first showers will arrive, signalling an end to the tourist season. Shack owners will dismantle their twenty-by-twenty-square feet coconut thatched paradises, and return to their villages to plant paddy. Tattoo parlours will pull down their shutters, and hippies like him will park their backpacks and trailer vans in other tropical climes. All of Goa will become empty and bereft of colour. And the skies will weep endlessly for the children who have disappeared.

But Goa being Goa, cannot be devoid of colour for long. The rains will bring with them colours of a different kind. Strange and exotic flowers will bloom over lush green hillsides. Sudden rainbows will slash the sky. Milky waterfalls will tumble down hillsides, inviting many a class-cutting student to an untimely death. And the second tourist season will begin.

The domestic tourist season.

'*Goa in the monsoons – a feast for your eyes*', the ads will proclaim from dailies and back pages of magazines. Enticing a different kind of tourist – the budget holidayer, lured by off-season rates. Honeymooning couples will stroll hand in hand on Calangute and Baga beaches, decked in almost wedding finery. North Indians who've never seen the sea, will splash in waist deep water, wearing Rupa underwear and banians – or worse – striped pyjama boxers. Bratty kids will insist on eating softie ice creams in pouring rain.

The tourism department and the hotels of Goa have been conning domestic tourists for too long. According to their brochures, the Goan monsoon is a sight for sore eyes. Only Goans know it is a *sore sight*.

Pouring incessantly, sheets of rain disrupt traffic and cause rivers to overflow. Filling streets and fields with muck and puddles, puddles that become happy hunting grounds for mosquitoes. The heat can drive people insane when combined with a power cut, of which there are plenty. Insects and large moths with bizarre patterns get attracted to house lights and street lamps. And sometimes, unwelcome visitors pay a visit.

One monsoon, Balgo stayed in Goa instead of returning to Australia. Every day he found a snake coiled underneath his kitchen stove. Even putting clothes in the laundry basket became a dangerous affair; scorpions would be residing there, having fled their underground homes inundated with water.

Tara gestures to a passing waiter for the bill. Balgo looks disappointed. "What's the hurry?" he asks, checking his wristwatch.

It's been their routine for nearly a month. At 10.30 p.m. they get up to leave. She pays the bill and they proceed to fetch their respective scooters. She always pays the bill even when he offers. "It's just coffee!" she says, sounding exasperated. Making a departure from this routine, Tara hugs him. They stay locked for a while. He is a bit unnerved; it is the first time she is displaying intimacy in public. People stare at a local girl shamelessly embracing an unkempt hippie. They disengage. He wonders what the matter is; she's only going on a holiday, within state limits.

On reaching her house, they park their scooters against the wide trunk of a mango tree. Lingering awhile beneath its sheltering canopy has become another routine. Propped against the tree they smoke a few joints. It's getting increasingly difficult to do this in the open. Even the beaches aren't safe. The cops and sniffer dogs are everywhere. Her orchard is a safe haven; no one can see them here. He sometimes kisses her, stoned little kisses. He does not push his luck, or hang around too much. Balgo is aware that Goans tolerate his kind so long as they stay out of their backyards, and their children's lives. One thing he's quite sure of. Tara will marry a nice local boy. Eventually. Not that he's harbouring hopes – he's not the marrying kind.

There's Gregory. Buzzing like a bee who has sacrificed his stripes. Tara will definitely marry him, even though she insists she cannot stand the sight of him. She is only fooling herself, or making small talk to distract him from reality. *His reality*. That he is just an exotic indulgence, her last carefree fling, partaken before plunging into domesticity: with four dogs, two kids, one husband and a house with a trap door. Just his luck he happened to be around.

He figured as much during the Carnival Float Parade when he saw them together. Fussing over Gregory, she was behaving like they'd had a lovers' tiff. What hurt him most was what she was wearing; the same red halter-top she'd worn at *his* trance party. The setting sun reflected off its sequins, tossing tiny points of light at him as he stood a few metres across from her on the opposite side of the street.

Tara looked through him, like he did not exist.

27

Tara's Dream

Reluctantly getting down to packing at 1.30 a.m., Tara lowers a small suitcase kept on top of her wardrobe. Thankfully she doesn't have to cart her SCUBA equipment; the office has already sent it to the Colva guest house.

Heeding Balgo's advice, she has spoken to a professional fish tank cleaner to clean her fish tanks once in two weeks. Dad has volunteered to feed her starfish every night, promising not to let Aajji snoop around in her rooms under the pretext of tidying up. Tara does one final check of all her fish tanks before going to sleep.

A faint knock rouses her. Lying motionless she listens, afraid to turn and look at the sliding windows in her bedroom. After few minutes of holding her breath and straining her ears, she drifts back to sleep. The same knock, now louder, and someone whispers close by. "Tara, wake up!"

She wearily gets up and opens the window, letting him enter inside her dream. "What is it now? Balgo, what do you want at this hour?"

His large palms are all over her body. "Hey!"

He has precise fingers. Within seconds their clothes are on the floor. Turning her around and pressing her against a large fish tank, he traces a path to the base of her spine. To the little area branded with her identity. He tattoos her afresh, this time more pleasurably, with his tongue. Over and over, so deliberately, so slowly, that she begs him to go further. Breasts and palms flattened against glass provide her starfish an extraordinary view. They watch fascinated at bodies rubbing and sliding, making sounds similar to a DJ scratching records.

28

Convalescing in Colva

The company guest house in Colva looks like a Spanish hacienda, with pale blue exteriors partly concealed by ivy. Trellis-covered windows placed liberally on the single-storied mansion provide ample parking space for seagulls and doves.

A profusion of hibiscus and bougainvilleas decorate the front porch, where sparrows chatter noisily on a broken birdbath. Seashells, corals and mother-of-pearl are strewn on steps leading to a veranda. A striped hammock sways forlornly.

Beyond the compound wall, Colva beach is a limpid turquoise, lapping at the horizon of a shamelessly cobalt sky. As Tara walks barefoot towards beckoning waves, pristine white sand feels like corn flour under her feet. In the distance, mackerel put out to dry on sand by local fishermen catch the overhead sun and glint like coins.

She returns to the guest house, changes into beach clothes and drags an easy chair to the balcony. She fetches a chilled beer from a well-stocked refrigerator. Like a good host, Mr Martin has taken care of everything.

Was it a bad idea avoiding all those office picnics, Tara wonders as she feels a sudden longing to meet the boys. She hopes for a miracle, like a barge going under – not with people, just cargo. Then the Martin boys will be forced to land up. But this is Colva, no barges pass by. The only visible oil is on bodies of middle-aged white tourists.

Hours turn into days as she learns to cherish her time-out at the company guest house. She trawls the beach for shells, goes snorkelling in the shallow reefs, swims till her limbs threaten to slip out of their sockets, and keeps the hammock happily occupied.

⚓

One morning Tara awakens to a slightly different day. The sky is dark blue, filled with thick clouds that obstruct the sun every few minutes, casting shadows that shift visibly over sea. It is a perfect day to catch starfish. This play of light and shade intensifies under water due to refraction, disorienting the sea creatures. She runs to the kitchen to look for a container, something to hold her captured starfish. A large jar of thick glass is filled with biscuits. To the consternation of the caretaker, she empties the biscuits on the kitchen counter and runs off with the jar.

Donning her fluorescent green bikini – bought so reluctantly – and orange flippers, she readies her equipment. Not having to dive in murky waters gives her a rare opportunity to abandon her wetsuit. She straps a single oxygen cylinder into a harness, wears her buoyancy control device and checks the pressure gauges and regulator valves. Slipping two knives into slots on either side of her weighted waist belt, she pulls her hair away from her face and ties it in a tight braid.

The local fishermen are already out at sea, taking advantage of the weather. She walks towards a fisherman readying his catamaran and enquires if he'll give her a ride. Impressed by her diving gear, he agrees. About two kilometres from the shore, she sees corals down below. Further ahead, some fishing boats are already pulling in their catch. An uneasy calm has befallen everywhere, except the fishermen; their hyperactivity reminiscent of a feeding frenzy among sharks. They have a short span of time to net their catch before a pre-monsoon storm comes raging in. Tara makes one final check of her equipment and dives in.

The visibility underwater feels surreal, like she's in a giant swimming pool. However, the twenty metre-all around-visibility is wasted as she cannot find a single starfish after an hour of searching. She calls off the search. Keeping aside ten minutes to ascend slowly, she witnesses a spectacular sight: drops of rain pockmark the surface of a tranquil sea, silver streaks slash it where lightning makes contact. Seeing lightning she imagines thunder, for down below is a soundless world. The rain begins to fall in long continuous sheets.

Unsuccessful at catching starfish, Tara finds solace in catching rain.

29

Bartender Serves a Molotov

Tara is a little worried. Balgo has not dropped by to collect his parcel. This was not supposed to happen. It was a surety – a bond he had signed, sealed and placed in her bag, the night before she left for Colva. She calls the Casa to enquire if he has left for Benaulim. Once again the phone rings till it disconnects – the tenth time this has happened in last three days. Where *is* everybody?

The Casa de Paraíso has fifteen to twenty guests at any given time. And they never shut, even during off season. Benaulim beach is two kilometres south of Colva. Tara decides to go for a walk, hoping to bump into Balgo. It's early evening; the shacks are filling with well-roasted charter tourists, glazing over their beer mugs. She scans every shack, describing Balgo to the bartenders. They direct her to a bar called By George; it's where backpackers usually hang out. It looks more hospitable than the temporary beach shacks.

Seeing a vacant stool at the bar counter, Tara walks in and sits. The bartender, a handsome sixtyish guy with salt and pepper hair, comes over.

"Youlookfamiliar, what'syourname?"

"Pardon?"

"I said, you look familiar. What's your name?"

"Tara Salgaonkar."

"My god! You've changed!"

Tara is no longer surprised how anyone in Goa can be a relative or a family friend.

"Good ol' Sukanya and Ramesh! How'sshedoin? And Ramesh's fruit business still top class?"

"Sorry I don't know you. Dad's fine, but Mom died ten years ago."

"*Died?*" he is aghast. "How...howdidithappen?" He's interrupted by a customer, "Stay, I'llbeback."

The bartender returns after a few minutes. He gestures to a waiter to take over.

"Sukanya died in Bombay?"

"Yes, ten years ago,"

"And I didn't know! Why Ramesh didn't call me… hope she didn't suffer?"

"Death was instantaneous."

"Was she ill?" the bartender probes further.

"Let's not discuss this…" Tara is fed up of the Goan habit of prying into everybody's lives. Random bartenders, especially, must be kept at bay.

"Sorry. What brings you to Benaulim? Taking a breather from Bombay?"

"Dad and I live in Saligao now, with Aajji. We left Bombay after mom's death. And I'm here because I'm staying at my company guest house in Colva."

"Oh you're here for work. Where d'you work?"

"Martins' Dredging."

"Whatd'youdo? Secretary?"

"No! Commercial diver."

His face lights up. "Sukanya must've been thrilled. She had big dreams for you…"

"Mom died before I got my licence and certification."

"Oh that is sad. Have a drink. On the house."

"You may be a family friend, but I don't know you."

"Tara, I'm your mother's boyfriend! Ok, ex-boyfriend. Leslie Fernandes. Sukanya used to call me Lez."

"Oh! Of course! She mentioned you many times. You guys made a trip to Goa to look for George Harrison," Tara says delightedly, her previous suspicion gone. "Was it true? I mean, mom told me all kinds of stories, most of them seemed cooked up," Tara shakes her head in disbelief.

"Absolutely true! I met George Harrison and promised him I'll open a beach bar in Goa one day, named after him."

Oh, I thought you spelt 'Boy' wrong," laughs Tara.

"*Shee-shee*, I don't like *that* George's music."

"Me too!" she laughs. "You knew my mom before she met my dad?"

"Yes, from Xavier's. She was my senior. I lived in Dhobi Talao, she lived in Grant Road. We got along well, being townies. Sukanya met Ramesh during that George Harrison trip. We lost touch after they got married. Couple of years later, I moved to Goa and got married. Your parents came for my wedding with you. You were a wee baby – and here you are, all grown up. Can't believe Sukanya's no more. How did she go?"

Tara bites her lips. "She… she committed suicide."

"What? I'm so sorry, I'm so sorry… Must've been terrible for you and Ramesh."

"It was, at that time…"

"Oh dear lord, she killed herself. Oh lord!"

"Ya, she did…"

"He's a good man, your father. He loved her so much, in spite of knowing. She could've told you, when you were old enough to understand, but she bottled it in for so many years. May Lord forgive her sins, grant her peace…"

"Oh, suicide is not a sin for us Hindus. Wait, what did you say? What should she have told me?"

"See that blue house over there, that's my home. Come, have dinner with my family. We'll talk."

"Some other time."

"I have to tell you, Tara. Listen carefully, okay?" He starts hesitantly, "I know why Sukanya committed suicide."

"Oh please, let's not get into that."

"You have to hear me out, Tara. Ramesh loved her so much – and he loved you too, like his own – still does, I can tell. She couldn't handle that; she was consumed by guilt."

"Loved me like his own?"

"I feel horrible saying this. Ramesh is not your real father."

Tara is taken aback. "How dare you!"

"You were conceived on that George Harrison trip, before she met Ramesh."

"What the fuck! George Harrison is my father?"

"No! Not him, his friend Richard, a hippie musician hosting him in Goa. Actually, my mistake. I fought with Sukanya that day, left her on the beach with that dreadlocked, green-eyed hippie. She hooked up with him just to spite me, I think."

"Enough! Mom would never do that. You're lying; you hate her because she chose my dad. Your free drinks are making me sick." Tara leaves the bar in a huff.

The darkness outside is a wall she has to break with every step. She tries to make sense of her conversation with the bartender.

Should she give it any importance? An excellent storyteller just like her mother. What if she calls her dad and confronts him? That'll be the best way to kill this hearsay. She soldiers on in the dark, rewinding the conversation in her head as she walks. *What did Leslie say? A dreadlocked, green-eyed hippie musician named Richard, who was hosting George Harrison, is her real father?*

And then, like a bolt of lightning, it hits her. The realisation sits in her stomach like a cannonball, till she can barely walk. Clutching her stomach, she falls to her knees. She finally understands why Aajji hated her mother all these years. *Because Aajji knew.* Her dad knew too. That Mom had cooed like a cuckoo, dropping her egg in *his* nest. A different egg he nurtured as his own, choosing to be blind to the difference.

Tara finally understands why her mother recounted tales of shamans and hippies. Of one hippie in particular. Was it her way of telling, by dropping hints? Tara bawls on the deserted beach. Suddenly all the jigsaw pieces fit, to reveal a horrible picture. *Of herself.* If only Mom had warned her to stay away from him instead of romanticising him, she would have listened.

And *he* had no idea that fateful night, that she is his daughter. Her eyes are actually his, and they are cursed. On her, they certainly are. As if she was given a choice. She has her mother's dark skin and his green eyes. In college she tried hiding behind dark glasses, even wearing black contacts, but her eyes watered like mad. Afraid that he would never be able to find her, if they were covered. And all the times they've met, their eyes recognised each other; they did not.

Sukanya's strange habits now make sense. Her obsession with sandalwood, for instance. When Tara was a child, she would only bathe her with Mysore Sandal soap. Oval-shaped and hard like a block of wood, it barely lathered. Sticking her nose into Tara's belly button, she'd say, "Mmmm, my little star, you smell so yummy!"

The kids at her swimming pool carried Lux and Camay, while Tara had to contend with Mysore Sandal soap. Everyone laughed at her. She hated it, hated the scent of sandalwood. If only she had known, her mother was tracing her lover's scent on his daughter's body. Holding on to his smell, because she could not hold on to him.

And then one night, a much older Tara returned with more than his scent inside her.

30

A Storm Rages Within

The weather bureau has forecast three days of continuous heavy showers with cyclonic activity. Outside her window, the wind howls through coconut trees. A restless ocean heaves and crashes violently against the shore. Dark clouds ferment on the horizon, stirred by quicksilver lightning bolts, turning the sky into a demonic cauldron.

Inside her room a wall calendar dances frantically, scratching a semicircle on the wall. Still a couple of weeks left for her to go home. But will Tara ever be able to go home now?

Balgo has not showed up. Maybe he didn't even mean to visit Benaulim. Maybe the parcel was just an excuse to meet her that night and embarrass her starfish.

The parcel. Tara has completely forgotten about its existence. It sits pretty at the bottom of her suitcase, out of sight and out of mind. Digging it out hurriedly, she keeps it on a table where she can see it at all times. Just seeing it annoys her. After making love to her the night before she left for Colva, Balgo had upturned her packed suitcase to conceal the parcel inside her clothes.

Tara slashes it with a knife. A stash of ecstasy tablets and joints fall out. It is the last thing she expected. A goodie bag of drugs to ease her stint at the company guest house. She starts hyperventilating, remembering how her taxi had been stopped at a *nakabandi*[25] in Margao, en route to Colva. A beat cop had recognised her and let her pass. What if he had searched her belongings? Sniffer dogs were there too, singling out tourists carrying drugs and booze as they headed to the South Goa beaches.

Tara flings the parcel outside her window and collapses on her bed feeling deflated. Why did she agree to carry it without asking what's inside? She assumed it would be some harmless trinket – a dream catcher wind chime or a sandalwood elephant.

She hasn't eaten anything since last night, when the caretaker left after a fight with her. Weak from hunger, she forces herself out of bed, opens the backdoor and heads to the kitchen. There is a casserole with chicken xacuti on the kitchen platform. She opens it. The smell reminds her of dead bodies. She walks back to her room, retrieving the joints and colourful tablets one by one, scattered like party confetti below her window.

Tara pops a few pills; it should keep hunger at bay for a while at least. Since morning, she's had a foreboding that Gregory will drop by. It's Saturday evening, he is most probably polishing his Enfield, all set for a ride. The last time she spoke to him – before leaving for Colva – he had threatened to surprise her, saying Mr Martin had given him keys to the Colva guest house. The first few nights, she barely slept, afraid of waking up and finding Gregory beside her. But when Balgo didn't show up, and the days began to meander, she started fantasising about that prospect. She hates herself.

---

25. Police checkpoint

Gregory is exactly the sort of man she is terrified of ending up with. Why did his narrow path swerve in her direction, *her* of all people? Perhaps like the early Jesuits who landed in Goa, he sees her as a heathen in need of reformation. And like his predecessors, he believes he's been handpicked for the job. Tara imagines the look on his face when he realises just how much more reformation will be required.

No use crying, she scolds herself as she lights a joint. The smoke mixes with her tears. The tear-laden smoke drifts outside a half open window at the foot of her bed, and turns into rain. Sneaking back inside, it sprays her gently. Suddenly a gust of wind smacks the window and a hinge comes loose, causing the window to open wide and rattle violently. A pair of sheer white curtains billow at her feet, like ghosts entering from dark skies. Just when they seem poised to enter, they are sucked out with a loud *thwhoop*. *'Fly away! Be Free!'* she beseeches them. They fall limply inside, giving up on the threshold, unable to go beyond to possibilities beckoning.

A familiar squawking sound alerts her. Soon it is near her window. The curtains part and a colony of seagulls enter her room. Tara has witnessed this spectacle a thousand times before – the frenzy provoked by a piece of edible floating garbage. The gulls circle hungrily, studying her, staking their claim. She winces as the pecking starts, sharp stabs detaching flesh from her bones.

In a few minutes, the waters will be clean.

31

Tara and the Deochaar

Tara has not answered his calls, her mobile has been switched off for the last few days. Even the Colva guest house landline rings incessantly and disconnects. Worried, Gregory informs Mr Martin. Mr Martin brushes it off. The caretaker is deaf, he says, and Tara must be at the beach all day. She does not return missed calls, period. But Gregory's gut feeling says something *has* gone wrong.

It's late evening when he arrives at the Colva guest house. It looks unoccupied, not a single light is switched on. Even the gate lamps are unlit. His spare key is useless, the main door is latched from inside. Walking from window to window, he calls out Tara's name. All windows are shut and thick curtains bar his view of the inside.

He sees an open window at the far end and runs towards it. A dull grey curtain hangs from a single hook, sodden with rain and dirt. Gregory climbs inside. Assisted by faint moonlight creeping through the window, he surveys the room. His heart skips a beat when he sees the bed. A ghostly figure lies stretched. Sickened by the apparition, his knees buckle. He has seen many a corpse in his stint as a navy diver, but none like this one. It is still alive. Nearly eight to ten kilos lighter, she's unrecognisable. Slowly turning her head, she stares at him.

Dusting the bed sheet, he sits beside her, sniffs the burnt stubs and the pills strewn around – proof that he's been right all along. He always suspected this about Tara; she's not someone who takes the long road to self-destruction. She flies there.

He lifts her and takes her to the kitchen; it's a mess and the fridge is empty. A loaf of bread on the granite platform looks quite mouldy, but it's all he can find. Buttering a slice he forces her to eat. He spots an opened carton of orange juice and puts some in a glass. Tara retches violently on drinking it. She starts frothing at the mouth. Gregory panics. He dials Carlos.

"Come to Colva right now. I'll text you directions to the company guest house."

"What for?"

"Tara is dying Carlos, please, just come!"

"What! Did you do something?"

"No way! Just get here, I'll explain later."

Gregory hates getting Carlos involved, but he cannot call Mr Martin. Nor can he call an ambulance, they'll ask him to register a police complaint.

Carlos arrives after an inordinately long time. Gregory rushes to his car with a swaddled up Tara and stretches her on the back seat. Then goes and sits beside Carlos, instructing him to drive to Mapuça city, to his family doctor's clinic. Carlos is horrified. He looks accusingly at Gregory, waiting for an explanation.

"Start driving!" orders Gregory.

"What happened?" Carlos asks.

"I don't know. She's not showered or eaten for weeks, taken drugs also, I think."

"Really?" Carlos acts surprised.

"Don't know why she did it," Gregory mutters. "It'll ruin her reputation."

"Reputation?" Carlos guffaws. "If she was awake, she'd say, 'What reputation-*sheputation?*'" He imitates her way of talking. Tara sits up from her foetal position and hits him hard on his head. A startled Carlos swerves off the road. Both men are stunned. Within seconds, she is back to her prone position, snoring softly. Gregory tries hard not to laugh. He is pleased with her reaction. As always, Tara will pull through this too.

Ten minutes pass in silence. "Does she consume regularly?" Gregory whispers to Carlos.

"Don't know," Carlos whispers back.

"From where she gets it?"

"Boss, this is Goa. Any five-year-old can tell you – that's if he's not a peddler himself." Carlos laughs in a considerably lowered volume.

"So she's got a regular peddler."

"I never said that."

"Don't protect her, Carlos. You know it's dangerous, especially for a diver."

"Drugs are bad for everybody, not just divers. Had no clue she does them. I'm as surprised as you, Gregory."

"This has to stop. I won't let her screw up her life like this."

Carlos puts an arm around Gregory's shoulder, "Look, it's not my business, but may I say something?"

"Sure."

"Do what's needed now and get the hell out. Trust me, I've learnt the hard way. God knows what her problem is, she'll never tell. You'll break your head trying to figure out," he pauses to breathe. "You know what, I don't think she's fully human – I mean, like a hybrid." He looks at Gregory, "I'm not joking! Who keeps such big fish tanks? For starfish? Bullshit! She sleeps in them! Daytime she's normal like us, at night she climbs inside those tanks and sleeps, I think. Must have gills or something. That's why she's better than us sods!" He's about to burst into another guffaw, but stops and looks behind.

Gregory asks him to stop the car.

"Carlos, step outside please."

"Why?"

"Just a sec…"

Gregory waits till Carlos is out of the cramped car, giving him enough room to take a swing at his aquiline nose. He breaks it. And hears a familiar giggle from the car.

Tara opens her eyes and sees fish tanks. She's lying on her own bed, in her own house in Saligao. So Colva didn't happen at all, it was just one long nightmare. Now that it's over, she can finally sleep.

"Tara? You awake? "

"Huh?"

"How you feeling? Can you get up and wear fresh clothes?"

Gregory's face is looming large above hers. Hasn't she seen this nightmare before? Are they showing her reruns now? Tara walks wearily to her wardrobe, locates a night-suit and goes to her bathroom to change.

"My family doctor refused to admit you to his clinic, he said go to Asilo or GMC. But he checked you and said it wasn't so bad. Mostly dehydration and starvation."

Tara interrupts, "Won't happen again, sorry..."

"What if I hadn't come to check on you? Tara, were you trying to kill yourself?" She does not reply or meet Gregory's gaze.

"Did you also inject yourself?"

"I *don't* like injections."

"Then what's this?" he asks, twisting her arm till she winces in pain.

"Mosquito bites!"

"STOP LYING, TARA."

"STOP SCREAMING, GREGORY."

Carlos butts in, "Gregory, she hates injections. She's shit-scared of them…"

"I carried a parcel for a friend. Didn't know what was inside… He was supposed to collect it, but he never came. I got curious and opened it. Found a cocktail of drugs. I was so angry that he tricked me into carrying them… thought I'd try *just a few*, you know to calm down and…"

"You didn't stop till you finished the entire packet," completes Gregory. "Tara, he was trying to kill you."

"What will anyone get by killing me?"

"Tell me his name. I'll report him to the police."

"Let it be, it's her personal business. Our job here is done," Carlos says to Gregory.

"Yes, please leave. I'm grateful to you Gregory; once again, you've saved me. You have this bad habit of showing up at the wrong time," she remarks and starts laughing. "Please just leave, both of you. I'm fine now."

It's almost dawn when they vacate Tara's house, leaving her with her starfish. The way it's meant to be. Waves of calm sweep over her as she watches them. Everything they need is within reach in their simulated environment. They have no wants – not that she knows of – and no desires. Desires are the root of all problems, her problems for sure. Lately she's been thinking of becoming like her starfish. *Asexual*.

The fish tank cleaner has done a wonderful job. Her starfish look healthy and the tanks appear cleaner than before. She wonders if they prefer the cleaner's touch to hers. Perhaps starfish have feelings too. Then her holiday must've hurt like abandonment. Do they ever feel lost, not knowing which limb to follow? Especially when each points in a different direction?

On the ceiling, light patterns reflecting from the tanks do an aquatic dance. She follows them with her eyes. Finding it difficult to keep pace, she gives up and falls asleep. A few hours later she awakens, soaked in sweat. There is a power failure; her room feels like an oven. She gets up and opens the sliding windows. A blast of cool breeze throws her off balance, harshly reminding her of her weight loss. The air reeks of wet earth and overripe mangoes. For the first time in ten years, Tara has missed the mango season. The orchard mangoes have been plucked, packed and delivered. Lying on the ground, rotting, are those that didn't make the grade. *Like her.*

She squints, adjusting her eyes to the darkness outside. The night is alive with a thousand teeny-tiny blinking lights. Not stars, fireflies! They come out to play when there's a lull in the rain. Nature's very own self-powered, light generators. During a power failure, or when the lights have all been switched off, a single firefly will enter her room and emit as much light as a zero watt bulb. The light is a signalling pattern to attract mates; an amorous Morse code. She marvels at the love play among her trees, wondering if her house also emits some kind of light. Drawing hapless mates into its lair. Feeding off their intense couplings.

Her gaze drifts towards a clump of trees. Lately she has noticed an apparition lurking there. She saw it for the first time in the early days of her three-month leave. It appears on successive nights behind a gnarled mango tree, fifteen metres from her window. To say she has actually seen it will be incorrect. It is intangible; she has merely sensed its presence.

One summer vacation, when Tara was ten, Aajji had told her a story of the *Deochaar*, a benevolent forest spirit and guardian of villages. He is immortalised in stone, with many a temple to his name, but there's no proof he actually exists. He guides lost people. Patrolling roads that pass through forests, he shows them the way if they stray. But heaven help those who turn around to peek at their benefactor. It angers him immensely. Screaming loudly, he recedes into the background, growing taller by the second, till he's taller than the tallest tree. Then he disintegrates into thin air.

Aajji spoke of relatives falling asleep at the wheel during their Bombay to Goa night trips, being awakened by a high-pitched scream. Rousing with a start, they had braked just in time before a ditch, a river embankment, or swerved from the path of a speeding truck.

But Tara was a rabid non-believer even at ten. "Science teacher says it's our imagination. There are no demons, ghosts or even Deochaars. Lack of sleep causes hallucinations."

An angry Aajji snapped, "Shut up and sleep, don't teach me."

As Tara grew older, the Deochaar stories reduced. She partly blamed the increase in traffic on the Bombay to Goa NH-17. Tarring of mud roads in villages, and the depletion of a once-dense forest cover had cemented the Deochaar's fate. He went into hiding. Unable to compete with bright sodium vapour

– streetlights kept highways and roads wide-awake, leaving no difference between night and day.

And after all these years of not believing in him, he decides to pay her a visit.

⚓

Tara understands his attraction to the orchard and her. He can hide among her trees *and* do his job. In a world filled with people who never seem to lose their way, she is someone whose default mode is set at 'lost'. But maybe he won't come tonight. Seeing Gregory and Carlos fussing over her, he may have assumed she's in capable hands, deferring his appointment to a later date. She will wait.

32

A Classic Tara Assignment

Tara is appalled to see her 'in' tray overflowing – estimates and bills have piled up in her absence. Hastily scribbled post-it notes instructing her to call various clients are stuck all over her soft board.

She corners Carlos. "Were you sleeping while I was gone?" Holidays are over for you guys, I'm back."

"What's the excitement?" Gregory butts in.

"Oh, hi Gregory. Good to see you as one of us," she tries not to sound too sarcastic.

"Thanks Tara. No work?"

"Carlos hasn't done any of the work he was supposed to."

"Mind your own work, Tara. I'll handle Carlos."

It strikes her like a slap. She's no longer the senior diver at Martins' Dredging Pvt. Ltd. Gregory Figueiredo is. Entering office, she carried on as if nothing had changed. Like hell it has.

Evaluations have taken place in her absence. From the prevailing happy mood, she presumes everyone's been rewarded according to their expectations. Just then Mr Martin's PA trots to her cubicle and says he wants to meet her. Leaning closer, she whispers, "Congrats Tara, you've been promoted too."

Too? To what, Tara wonders as walks down the corridor. Gregory is inside, discussing some papers. He stops talking on seeing her.

"Tara! You're back! " exclaims Mr Martin, "but… you don't look well. Did you fall ill at Colva? You've lost weight."

"Viral fever. It was raining."

"Oh dear… were you ill throughout?"

"Just towards the end," she says. Gregory shuffles uneasily in his seat.

Mr Martin smiles at her. "Welcome back, Tara. We have good news. Tell her, Gregory."

"Congratulations, Tara!"

Gregory hands her a letter. It says: "You are promoted to a Senior Supervising Diver". She reads it again. Like a cryptic clue it eludes her still vacationing brain. Is she expected to dive or supervise? "You will make evaluations of assignments and projects. Raise estimates and make project reports. You will delegate all work to the diver most suited for it. He will follow your guidelines and instructions. All decisions on assignments are subject to approvals from you."

"In simple English, tell me what this is."

"It's quite clear, Tara." Gregory gets defensive.

"*Patraos, me no comprendez…*"

"I was checking your records, Tara. You've suffered Type I DCS every two-three months. Not to mention one Type II during Andalusia…"

"Explain letter, not health record."

"Getting to it, patience Tara!"

"Since you're checking, check my successes rate on assignments also. It's 100%."

"Your health and safety record is being discussed, not performance. Tara, if you continue like this, you'll die before your time."

"I'd rather die of a nitrogen build up in my blood stream than cholesterol."

"This is what I… *we* don't like, this attitude of yours, Tara," Gregory slips into his patronising tone. Devoid of his navy uniform, it lacks potency. "We think you're becoming irresponsible," he continues, looking at Mr Martin for support. "We think you're setting a bad example for the team."

"Who's *we*?"

"Mr Martin and me."

Tara looks at Mr Martin accusingly, "So the two of you have decided I'm bad for the team. Just do me a favour, fire me!"

"C'mon, Tara…"

"Don't want this… this bullshit promotion. I'll go join another firm and start again as a rookie. At least I'll get to dive and not have to make estimates for the rest of my life."

"Who says you have to stop diving?" Gregory says to her.

Mr Martin takes over. "Tara, you say you hate paper work, but your estimates and project evaluations are perfect. Suppliers and vendors don't entertain me when I ask for discounts; they only want to talk to you. Clients love your project reports and pass them immediately…"

She starts laughing. "Suppliers-vendors give me good rates because I bargain like I'm buying *kanney-batatey*[26] – which I never buy. And clients pass my estimates because they want to

26. Onions-potatoes (Konkani)

see me work in body-fitting wetsuits. It's why you hired me, no?" she says, looking out the window at the Port. "Have you printed new visiting cards already? I'll leave right now."

"You're overreacting as usual, Tara," says Gregory. "Let's talk after lunch, just you and I. Mr Martin, I'll handle this."

"That won't be necessary, Gregory," Mr Martin shows him his place. "Tara, I brought you up from a rookie. I know you better than anybody. I thought you're ready for a different role. I mean, at some point you've got to stop diving. Instruct others to do what you want. That way you'll not wear out your body. I want you to get into management – like Gregory. But I was wrong. You are not ready, and may never be. Sorry. No bullshit promotion, you'll get an increment."

Tara is too upset to work, just imagining how they almost trapped her into becoming a form-filler, file-pusher! She needs to scream her head off. Only that will make her feel better. Balgo is the only one due for it. Dialling the Casa number, she quickly rehearses what to say.

Bholenath Guruji answers the phone. She is dumbstruck. Shouldn't she have prepared for this, considering the telephone is in *his* house? Tara furiously defaces an estimate with her doodling. After a minute of complete silence, she says hello again.

"Hi Tara, how're you?"

Not too well, and I deserve it. "I…I…I'm fine Bholenath Guruji. How're you?"

"Super! Just got back from Africa. Met tribal musicians, went on safaris, had a blast…"

"Wow! You went to Africa."

"Off season I catch up with the music world. How was your break, Tara?"

"It was okay. Balgo was to meet me in Benaulim, but he didn't show up. Is he okay?"

"Balgo? He's in Australia! I thought you knew."

"Australia? When did he go?"

"Four weeks ago. For the Aboriginal Arts & Music Convention at Ulluru Rock. In fact, I'm leaving tomorrow. We got a last minute invite."

"Oh! He could've just told me, I wouldn't have waited."

"Didn't he call you, Tara?"

"No."

"Maybe he couldn't get through."

"Maybe… So, when does he return?"

"Difficult to say… he hasn't seen his parents in a while. I think he'll stay for six months."

"Six months!"

"He's gone home after four years."

"Oh, ok. Thanks for telling me, Guruji. And…" she hesitates, looking for something to hold on – she's shaking. "I'm so sorry, Guruji."

"For what?"

"For… for calling you at this time. Disturbing your siesta."

"Not at all, I was packing. Take care, Tara, and cheer up. I'll tweak Balgo's ears and make him call you from Australia, I promise."

Will she ever muster the strength to really apologise? For now it seems fitting that she has to spend the rest of her life signing estimates and filing bills. It's her karma-sharma biting her bum.

⚓

Opening a file bulging with important papers, Tara takes one and folds it into a paper plane. Walking to a window, she launches it, watching the paper plane dip and dive just like she does underwater. Must be one of her estimates. She folds another – the file has to be cleared by evening. The phone rings, distracting her. Reluctantly, she shuts the window and goes to answer. Someone from the River Navigation Authority is hyperventilating.

"We insist you do it, Ms Salgaonkar; it's a tough assignment."

Tara smiles; long time since anyone said that. "I can't, I'm a supervisor now. Not allowed – I'll check with my – Okay, I'll do it! But my bosses won't like it."

"Ms Salgaonkar, for us, you're the boss. You just say yes, we'll handle the rest. Orders from top, only you should do it."

"Fine, I will!"

⚓

Earlier in the morning, a car had rammed into the side railings of the old Mandovi Bridge. A small section gave way, plunging the car into the river below. Aside from a few feet of missing railing, and skid marks on tarmac, there is no indication of an accident having occurred.

By afternoon, vividly coloured petrol splotches surfaced on water, appearing in a circle below the bridges.

Still, nobody suspected a thing. The Mandovi river is a regular waterway for ships and barges. They indulge in their own spilling of diesel and petrol every day. By evening, the tide washed ashore notebooks and foolscap pages.

Meanwhile, two sets of parents lodged a missing complaint. Their sons had left home at 6 a.m. for college but did not return at their usual time. The police, on fishing out the notebooks, found the boys' names on them. That's when they realised there was a lot more hidden in the waters. And now they've handpicked her to excavate and deliver the treasure to its rightful owners – parents.

A classic Tara assignment!

River Mandovi falls under jurisdiction of the Captain of Ports Department and the River Navigation Authority. It is busier than the highways of Goa. Search operations will have to be conducted cordoning off as little an area as possible.

At 11.30 p.m., Tara arrives at Panjim Jetty with her equipment. The Coast Guard ships are waiting, flooding the area underneath the bridges with searchlights. The Coast Guard divers have already earmarked her search area with buoys. She gets her diving equipment and metal cutters ready. It's not going to be a pretty sight down there. If the bodies have not surfaced yet, they are probably mangled and trapped in metal.

Diving into the turbid Mandovi waters, not too deep, but polluted, Tara tackles her toughest assignment since Andalusia.

33

Trapped in a Bell Jar

The river is pitch-dark. Tara has to position herself directly under Pier 2 on the Panjim side of the bridge – it's where the car wreck is. Carefully avoiding a section of the original collapsed bridge that still lies submerged. The original bridge had collapsed way back in 1986; the authorities have still not cleared a part of the debris. A three metre portion with rusted iron rods is visible during low tide. She often worries about people jumping off the bridge near that section. The poor sods will be skewered to death. Not that death by drowning is any less painful.

The water, swollen with garbage and oil, makes it difficult to read her nightglow compass. Suddenly her hand touches something soft and gooey, sending shivers up her spine. She is engulfed by a wall of mud, awakened from its decade long slumber on the pier. Moving twenty paces to her left should now land her in the backseat of the car.

One… two… three… four… twenty.

No backseat, no car. Tara has done it yet again! Retracing steps to where she started, she tries once more to her other left. At number eighteen, she grazes her left thigh against something sharp. Found the car! Covered completely in mud, it is impossible to tell what colour it is.

Like a blind woman reading Braille, she fixes underwater lights, putting cables into connecting slots. Doing everything right and yet, there is no light. The occupational hazards of an atheist diver. No one to say "Let there be light!".

Without wasting a moment and precious oxygen, she pulls out her emergency radium sticks and breaks them. Illuminated by the eerie greenish glow, and the faint beam of her own headlamp, she sees them, hands and faces pressed against rolled up windows.

Swimming to the windows, Tara caresses each of their faces through the glass. Telling them the wait is over, she is here now. In a few hours, they'll be free. She begins her task, wondering if they're amusing themselves while she labours. Playing with the condensation formed on window glass by their non-existent breath. Drawing hearts, scribbling names, tapping fingers impatiently, and urging her to speed up.

No, that is the tap-tapping of the metal cutter in her hand.

When Tara was three, she had accompanied her mother to a hospital. Sukanya went in for a consultation, while Tara waited outside. Seated on a bench, she observed the hospital. Wooden shelves with massive bell jars and test tubes lined the walls. Some were amber, some clear; all filled with a peculiar smelling liquid. Only years later in her school biology lab would she be re-introduced to that smell: Formaldehyde.

Those jars and test tubes held an assortment of body parts: infant hearts, infant brains, infant lungs and livers. Tara got up to do a little inspection – a three-year-old hardly knows how her insides look, or that they are supposed to be a gory sight.

She stopped at a wooden table. Six bell jars stood on it. Between them, they had foetuses in various stages of development. She thought they were monkey babies, till she saw the largest – a one-year-old male child. He was pale yellow and wrinkled. Feeling sorry for the babies, Tara looked around for someone to release them from their plight. Was this how parents collected babies from hospitals? They placed an order and when it was ready, like the fellow in the last jar, they came to fetch? So, where were his parents? Shouldn't someone remind them it was time to take the poor fellow out?

Tara's mother came along and enlightened her. "They're all bad babies, so they've been punished and put inside jars. They cannot come out and play."

"So sad, mummy!"

"Be a good girl, Tara, nobody will put you in a jar," her mother said to her as they walked out of the hospital. Tara yanked her little hand from her mother's grip and ran back inside.

"Mummy, I'm going to open those jars and set them free."

Tara cuts through the car framework that has collapsed in, crushing with it their tender teenage bodies. Everything is absolutely still; the only sounds are the dull whirring of her drill, punctuated now and then by mud-laden exhaust bubbles spewing from her breathing apparatus. She frees body parts and packs them in separate polythene bags, stamped with her company name. These bags, labelled and sealed, will be sent to the morgue at GMC Bambolim. Its contents preserved there until the police and the coroner's formalities are complete.

Four hours and she is done. Back where she belongs, doing what she does best.

34

Mr Matchmaker Martin

News travels fast in slow Goa. After the Mandovi river search operation, Mr Martin is bombarded with calls from angry clients demanding to know why he is still sending his bungling juniors, when the experienced lady diver is back.

He's happy with the way Tara handled the Mandovi river assignment, taking quick decisions, not wasting time on useless protocol – hallmarks of a Master Diver. And that's what he is going to promote her to, very soon. It's the least he can do for making her a supervisor, for one day. *Just one day!* But will she ever forgive him?

And then there's Gregory. It's obvious he envies Tara; even hates her guts. She seized an assignment that could've easily been his. But he chose to go home on time that day. Tara, who was working late, landed the perfect opportunity.

Mr Martin wonders why they aren't getting married – why none of his divers are getting married. Take him, for instance; marriage has helped him immensely. A loving and understanding partner to return home to after a gruelling day at work, actually increases the life span of a diver. The average burnout rate in this profession is thirty-seven, and Tara will get there soon. Even Gregory – except, he's had it easier as a naval diver. His wear and tear has just begun, now that he's with Martins'.

Then again, a married Tara may be pressured by in-laws and her husband to give up diving. To settle into domesticity, bear children and all those things expected of women. And what a colossal waste it would be! The day is not too far when she'll walk into his cabin with downcast eyes and shyly hand him her wedding invite.

The atmosphere at Martins' Dredging has reverted to the good old days, before Gregory was hired as Chief Diver. But something *is* different; Tara has changed. No longer interested in being anyone's boss, she has stepped back, withdrawn her cards so to speak. As if getting ready to quit the game.

He noticed this change after her return from Colva, and he is to blame. Triumphant at snagging a top-notch naval diver, he overlooked her. Taking away her authority and the respect she had earned from her subordinates, and handing it to Gregory on a platter. But Tara being Tara circumvented the situation in no time, reclaiming everything twice over.

It's been four months since her return from that enforced break. She's on top of all her assignments, and yet she looks deflated. Her stubbornness has mellowed, cheekiness gone. Even the secretaries have stopped being rude to her. It's like the old Tara has disappeared, and in her place is a milder, more polite replica.

Mr Martin wonders if he's being unusually alarmist. It could just be that Tara has decided to slow down. She is finally maturing. Hasn't he waited long enough for this to happen? He calls her to his cabin; he has some ideas to discuss.

"Tara, I'm hiring an assistant to do your paper work. After every assignment, brief him and go home. Of course, you'll need to train him in all the form-filling, report writing, bills despatch, etc."

Her eyes light up. "Excellent idea, Mr Martin! Do it for every diver."

"I can afford only one right now, for you and Gregory. Let's see how this works before we implement it for everybody."

"Thank you, Mr Martin! I'll have so much free time! Two hours a day go in paperwork."

"Great! Now you can get a hobby. "

"I already have one, Mr Martin."

"Oh Tara, that's a headache not a hobby! Something easier. Learn music. My nephew gives piano lessons."

"Piano-*shiano*'s so boring! Everybody in Goa plays piano or keyboards. If I learn an instrument, it'll be something unusual," she says, displaying shades of an earlier Tara.

"What do you fancy, Miss Tara? A Didgeridoo? It's an Australian instrument… heard one last year on my trip to Sydney. Funny looking thing, makes a weird sound too."

Tara's eyes well up and she immediately leaves his cabin.

Did he say something wrong? Mr Martin cannot understand what's up with her. Whatever it is, is giving him sleepless nights. He wonders if her folks are planning an arranged marriage or something. Or pressurising her to take a bank job.

The solution to Tara's problems walks right into his cabin. Gregory.

He's overheard the office secretaries gossip about Gregory and Tara. Of course, he hasn't given it much thought. Being the only female working alongside six males, Tara's been linked to all of them by turns. And now that Gregory is her seventh male colleague, it is his turn. He wonders what will happen if they *actually* start seeing each other. Not for a platonic after work coffee; more seriously. What if they get married? Then Tara could continue working as Gregory will not have an issue with her diving. Perfect!

Mr Martin decides to get his plan rolling. "There you are. What you doing after work, both of you, I mean?"

"Not much," they say in unison.

"We'll have coffee somewhere and go home," Gregory elaborates.

"I'm taking you out for dinner tonight, at Panjim Marriott."

Tara looks at him suspiciously, so he elaborates, "It's been a good month, thought I'd celebrate with the two people responsible for it."

"Marriott's a stuck up place," she says, making a face.

"Somewhere else then? Where would you like to fleece me? I'm in a generous mood today."

"Gregory, why don't you decide? I'm okay with any place that serves good seafood."

"Brenda makes the best fish curry in Goa. See, I got this belly after marrying her." Mr Martin rubs it, looking enviously at Gregory, thinking… *you lucky bastard, Tara can't cook, you'll maintain your washboard abs if you marry her.* "But I haven't told her, so let's keep that program for some other time."

"Any place is fine, Mr Martin," says Gregory.

"O Coqueiro? My brother-in-law is their manager. Nice live music they have," he says, looking at Tara.

"O Coqueiro? It's famous for that gangster incident. A Bombay cop caught him – whats his name? Charles Sobhraj! Madhukar Zende trapped him, by posing as a local. Am I the only one in Goa who's not been there?" asks Tara excitedly.

"Me neither," says Gregory.

Mr Martin's brother-in-law receives them at the entrance. They walk past the verandah – where Sobhraj is immortalised with a statue. Gourmand Gregory takes charge of the menu. After an order has been placed for fried calamari, stuffed crabs, pork sorpotel, beef tongue, chicken xacuti, steamed rice and some chilled beers, Mr Martin pops the question.

"Have you two decided about your future with Martins'?"

Tara looks nervously at Mr Martin, "What have I done now? Haven't got the bends even once in the last four months."

"Thank you, my dear. I meant, how long will you stick around?"

"Just joined six months ago," replies Gregory.

"Point I'm trying to make is, will the two of you be employees only, or take on bigger responsibilities?"

"Am I not a Joint Partner, Mr Martin?" asks Gregory. Tara looks surprised. This information was withheld from her.

"You have very little stake, Gregory. I still call the shots. I want to stop doing that, and..."

"And?" asks Tara, "Are you going to adopt Gregory?"

"No. But I know you've received feelers from other firms," he says, putting Tara on the back foot. "It's a small world Tara, especially our field."

"Mr Martin, if I *do* leave, I'll start my own company. Or become a contract diver. Ya! Definitely a contract diver... people can call me when they need me."

"Like a contract labourer? No medical, no insurance, no PF. A glorified *ghatti* you want to be, Tara?" Mr Martin scolds her. "You won't be fit and young all your life."

Tara looks suitably chastened. The evening is proceeding just the way Mr Martin has planned.

"I want to retire in a year, earlier actually. I have no children, I'll be very happy if the two of you manage my business for me. I'm proposing a three-way partnership, 50-25-25. 50 is mine," Mr Martin stops to check if they're processing it. "Now, between the two of you, you can make it a joint 50. Together, become equal partners with me. Choice is yours."

"What do you mean?" asks Gregory.

"He wants us to get married," says Tara, in a low voice.

"Correct! Am I wrong in suggesting it? You like each other, and you make a great team. And Tara, if you marry a non-diver he'll force you to stop diving. Gregory cannot – I'll break his neck if he tries! Take my advice, marry each other. Take charge of Martins' Dredging and let me retire."

"Consult your parents," Mr Martin tells Gregory. Turning to Tara he says, "What do you say, Tara?"

She looks outside the restaurant window. "Lightning just struck twice in the same place."

35

Balgo's Humble Abode

"Hello starfish."

"Hey! Where you calling from?

"Goa!"

"Really?" she asks, not so enthusiastically.

"Let's meet? Right now?"

"No! It's a working day! Got a big assignment at the Port. Tomorrow?"

"Okay. How're you? What's up?"

"Good… work as usual."

"Ahh, of course. Call me whenever you're free. Okay bye."

It's been so long, she has forgotten how he looks. Having sat out the miserable Goan monsoon in Australia and just as a pleasant December rolled onto Goan shores, he's back.

Balgo is back.

The temptation to continue from where they had left is immense. But meeting him will mean regressing to an earlier life best left behind; when she lived for and in the moments spent with him, sharing long silences, and sometimes conversations, over steaming cups of black coffee. She was on a break then. It was okay to behave that way.

She has responsibilities now; targets to meet, bottom lines to mind.

What would she do for a glimpse of his tattoo.

There's no assignment at the Port. Tara leaves office abruptly. On reaching home, she skips dinner. After a hot shower, she flops on her bed with wet hair, wet body, an empty stomach growling like crazy, and cries herself to sleep.

A loud knock rouses her. Hastily slipping on a t-shirt, she goes to open the door expecting Aajji with her portion of dinner.

Tara extends her hand and says exasperatedly, "Just give it." Something cold is placed in her palm. A pair of keys. Tara opens her eyes. *Holy shit!*

"I-I thought it was Aajji with dinner…"

"You have dinner at 2 a.m.?"

"It's 2 a.m.?"

"Ya."

"Okay, so?"

"So go change, I want to take you someplace," he says.

"Now? It's almost dawn. I have an early morning assignment at the…"

"Port?"

"Balgo, I *really* want to sleep."

"We'll be back soon."

Tara makes him push his Bajaj for close to a kilometre, and *then* lets him kick start. As they pass Nagoa and head towards Arpora hills, she leans forward from her pillion seat and tries to press the brakes.

"Stop! I'm not coming to that club on the hill. You're dragging me to a rave at 3 a.m.? Told you enough of times, I'm not doing that anymore."

"Relax, Tara. That's not where we're going."

They stop at an old house on a parallel hill. Balgo opens the gate and parks his scooter in the compound. "Come in," he says, walking towards the house. Opening the door with the same keys, he goes inside and switches on a dim light at its entrance. Standing on the *balcão*, his dreadlocks backlit, he looks very pleased. The house has a high roof, large doors and windows. The windows are particularly intricate; they have geometrical patterns made with red and green stained glass, adding the only touch of colour to the freshly whitewashed house.

She steps inside hesitantly. There is no furniture, just two unopened cartons in one corner. Standing in the centre and spreading his arms wide, he says, "My humble abode."

"How come?" Tara asks, quickly realising how lame it sounds.

"Can't live forever at the Casa. I've finally decided… this is it, Goa is home."

"What can I say… congratulations?"

"Don't like it, Tara?"

"It's really nice. Especially love the windows…"

He touches her cheek and a tear rolls down his finger. He pulls her closer and gives her a hug. "I missed you too, Tara. Sorry I took so long. I deejayed at some Sydney night clubs and sold my ancestral land for money to buy this house. Had my eyes on it for a long time."

Next morning, Balgo wakes up and finds her staring at him, eyelids all swollen. She had sobbed silently when he reclaimed her last night. "Whatchu doin?" he asks, tracing her eyelids with his finger. She shuts her eyes and shuts him out.

"Saving this on my hard disk," she says, opening her eyes.

"Huh?"

"This moment… light from that window, painting our bodies with triangles of red and green… so beautiful, it hurts."

"Oh Tara, my drama queen! You can have this moment every morning!"

36

The Wedding Rehearsal

Ramesh Salgaonkar fixes the date. There will be two ceremonies, one Hindu and one Catholic, a week after Easter. Tara is upset; she'd rather walk to the marriage registrar's office than walk down the aisle. Holding a white gossamer-like gown, she throws a tantrum, "It's a fancy-dress costume for the ice queen."

"Why didn't you go shopping with Gregory's family? Gave your measurements and left it to them," Ramesh reprimands her. "Now wear it!"

"Why two saris? What if they catch fire when I'm going round and round that square thingy?"

"Square thingy? My god, Tara, it's called *havan*!"

"Seven rounds around a havan gets you a lifetime in hell!" She guffaws.

Ramesh spies her sitting on the floor one afternoon, bewildered by a bundle at her feet. Fifty saris Aajji has collected over the years are tied in a white muslin cloth. It was stashed away in an old wooden cupboard in the main house. Some belong to his late wife Sukanya, some are Aajji's, and some have been bought especially for Tara, without her knowledge.

Aajji pulls out a huge metal trunk from underneath her bed. Opening it, she proudly shows Tara the contents – a collection of kapiyaalis made for her trousseau. That's when it finally sinks in. His daughter is getting married.

On the island of Chorao, preparations are in full swing. It's a first wedding for the Figueiredos too. The older son had eloped, opting for a civil marriage in a foreign land. But Gregory has chosen the honourable way – even if he is marrying a Hindu. They are planning a grand wedding, the grandest their little island has ever seen. A huge *matto*[27] is being constructed for the reception by the river. Exotic flowers are being flown in from

27. shamiana

Bombay florists. Gregory's uncle, Benny Da Costa, is in charge of catering.

And Marcus is invited.

This is big news for Chorao, bigger than the wedding. Everyone is looking forward to the prodigal's return, after nearly four decades in Portugal.

The vows will be exchanged at the Mae de Deus church in Saligao, not Gregory's church – Our Lady of Grace. Aajji manipulated the Figueiredos, citing her old age and ill health, to have the wedding closer home. Mae de Deus holds a special significance for Ramesh; it is where he accidentally met his wife, Sukanya.

As her wedding day draws near, Tara is still immersed in her assignments.

"Aajji is running around doing all the work," Ramesh complains.

"Dad, it is extra work she has created for herself, let her sort it. Besides, this is her swan song. I don't want to stand in the way of her performance."

Ramesh bursts out laughing. "So mean, Tara. Just be around; don't behave like these are your last days at work. You're going to continue after marriage, right? Wait, did Gregory say something?"

"He dare not!"

Ramesh is afraid he'll miss the very things that irritate him. Lights switched on through the night in her house, fights with Aajji at breakfast over electricity bills, strange music wafting into his orchards at odd hours, weekends filled with sounds of splashing water and squeaking glass.

"Tara, what about your fish tanks?"

"What about them?"

"You're taking them with you, no? They're the only dowry Gregory will get."

"He doesn't want; no space in his house."

"Oh! So then?"

"I'll come on weekends to clean them. What to do, Dad?" Should I give them away to the aquarium shops in Panjim?"

"No, let them be," he says, squeezing her shoulder. "I'll feed your starfish every night. At least this way you'll come back on weekends."

"Are you sure Dad?"

"Absolutely!"

⚓

On the afternoon of her wedding rehearsal, Ramesh gets a call. "It's an important client, Dad. I have to do it. I'll miss the rehearsal, but I'll be home for the big dinner."

"Oh! Come on Tara, tell someone else to do it."

"Only Gregory or I can. But it's my client… talk to Gregory," she says, handing the phone to him.

"Mr Salgaonkar, I'm leaving office now. I'll go home first and get my family. We'll be at the church by 7 p.m. The wedding planner is coming on her own."

"And the bride-to-be? Isn't she required?"

"Uncle, it's just a rehearsal, we are doing it so all of you understand how things happen in a church wedding. As the father of the bride, you will have to learn your cues. My family and relatives know their parts. I'll explain to Tara what she needs to do."

"Give the phone to her," Ramesh tells Gregory. "Tara, I don't like what you're doing. This is not the way to treat one's own wedding."

"Dad, this is absolutely the last assignment, I swear. Nothing after this. Please let me keep my commitments. Everybody gets married; the world shouldn't be put on hold, no?"

Tara was cribbing about the rehearsal right from the start, infuriating the priest by commenting, "Why rehearse? All I have to say is 'I do'. Any cretin can do that."

She finds her excuse, not to.

37

Starfish Pickling

Stepping inside the pond, Tara can tell right away it will take her three hours.

Of late, she has learnt to appreciate the monotony of a de-silting, de-cluttering her mind as she scrubs and scrapes on autopilot. Almost like yoga or meditation – something she'll never do, preferring a visit from Mr Rigor Mortis to one from Mr Ramdev. Tara likes to call it blanking out.

Blanking out is a technique her swimming coach had taught her. He would insist all swimmers attend practice even during final exams, much to the ire of parents. "It will help them study better," he'd say. After doing sprints, they had to round off the day's session with laps – two kilometres non-stop. Coach would instruct them to remember the day's incidents while counting laps, and visualise them dissolving in water. Before they knew, their breathing synchronised with strokes, and their minds emptied of useless thoughts. They left the pool an hour later, physically tired but mentally fresh.

Tara badly needs this de-silting to empty her mind of earlier memories; to start afresh.

She zeroes in on her most difficult memory – *Finding Bholenath Guruji.*

The second time, that fateful night in Colva. She curses herself for having had blinders on during the first time. Now there's one more scab to peel. And she'll have to continue being the lone pallbearer for her mother.

Balgo.

Should she move into his life? And his beautiful house on Arpora hill? The prospect seems tempting, but it will be selfish on her part. And far too easy. She has to let go. *Let him go*, even though he doesn't want to. He is destined for bigger things. He doesn't know it yet.

A few water hyacinths have reared their ugly heads. Tara quickly plucks them. She is pleased to see the lotuses doing well.

They looked so beautiful that night of the trance party.

Small quantities of silt have blocked the mouth of the spring. Tara scrapes it off, freeing the sand to its original buoyancy. It rushes towards her in gratitude. The beam of her headlamp traps the tiny particles in its path, illuminating each with a halo. A delicate drizzle of muddy rain settles over her wetsuit. She is bound by mud; it casts a spell on her. A dusty granite statue in a forgotten underwater ocean park, having stood still for ages, shrugs off its stillness, stops being spellbound, and gets on with work.

⚓

Tara gazes at the night sky. There are no stars above. Almost as if a thick black shroud has hidden them from her view. Reaching out for them, she returns empty handed. Even the stars have forsaken her tonight. Floating on her back, she remembers something.

After that night in his new Arpora house, she was unable to face Balgo. Afraid to look back while her life was on a forward moving path, with Gregory. But the days passed, and with every passing day, it became easier to forget. Her wedding date got fixed, and she got swept into the excitement – it was difficult not to, even for her.

Then something happened, something she had not anticipated, even though it was the most natural thing to happen. And it happened despite all the precautions one takes to *not* let it happen. As they say, life has a way of bursting forth, especially when you try to stop it. Like a microscopic seed that falls into a tiny crack on a wall, firmly implants itself and becomes a mighty peepal, taking over the entire house.

Tara was wracked with guilt. *Not again!* she told herself. All these years of being careful, and yet, she slipped. She wondered if she should inform Balgo that she was carrying his child. She felt she owed him an explanation – not that he would ever ask for one. So she wrote him a letter. Next morning, she left home earlier than usual. Taking a detour on her way to work, she went to his house and pushed the letter underneath his door.

Balgo's Bajaj was parked outside; he was still sleeping. As she turned to leave, she saw the view from the topmost step of his house, and gasped.

That night it had appeared like a bottomless dark chasm. Illuminated now by the early morning light, the view was breathtaking. All of Arpora, Nagoa, Parra, Pilerne and Saligao stretched below. The Arabian Sea shimmered on the western horizon, as dawn broke over the east. Tara felt like she was standing on the edge of the world. Descending the steps, she walked to the edge of *his* world, and looked down.

Nah! It wasn't time to fly. Besides, she prefers the ocean to the sky.

She imagines Balgo reading her letter, and smiles at the thick blanket of darkness above. He smiles back at her, calling her a lousy love-letter writer. He had once asked her why she collects starfish, and she replied she had reached for the stars and got starfish instead. As always, she blurted something without understanding its true meaning. Much later, in Colva, the realisation dawned. That day, she became desperate to see him, to tell him she finally understood…

Starfish in the ocean
Are stars on probation,
When starfish die
They become
Taras in the sky…

"Don't laugh, just read my letter," Tara says to the dark, starless night.

My dearest Balgo,

You entered the pond that magical night and I just knew you'd be the one reading this letter. I've merely put on paper what was written long ago, even before you showed up in my life. You see, Balgo, history has a weird way of repeating itself. And while I hate all talk of karma-sharma, even I could not stop myself being entangled in it. I see now, as clear as the waters I will never swim in, I see how I wilfully played along all the while.

I judged my mother for the life she gave me, the circumstances in which she bore me, and I became her. Living her exact same life, over and over... But now I have a choice before me. And I choose to end it, with me. It stops here, it stops now. Karma and sharma can go fuck themselves.

Don't be afraid, Balgo. I'm not asking you to do anything – it's already done. I'm merely entrusting you with a recipe. I've been making it for years now. In fact, it's become a part of me, and I suspect I've become a part of it too. Someday, if you wish, you may hand it down to someone you love. But imbibe it thoroughly. For I have.

STARFISH PICKLE

Ingredients:

- 1 kg firm starfish
- 2 tsp ground turmeric
- 3 cups vinegar
- 25 dried Portuguese chillies
- 1 tablespoon cumin seeds
- 2 inch piece fresh ginger
- 1 head of garlic
- Oil
- Salt to taste

Method:

Clean starfish and test their mettle in boiling water for forty-five minutes. De-skin.

Rubbing salt and turmeric on their skinless body removes the fishy smell. Set aside for an hour.

Grind spices, garlic and ginger, in a little vinegar. Fry starfish until tender. They are tough, resilient creatures; it takes effort to soften them. But when they do soften up, they are wonderful.

Fry masala for a few minutes, then add remaining vinegar. Mixing of sour and spice will release a pungent aroma. Prepare for tears in your eyes. Cook for ten minutes on low heat.

When starfish and masala cools down to room temperature, place starfish in a pickle jar and top up with masala/vinegar mixture.

Cover lid tightly with white cheesecloth.

Consume after setting aside for one year.

Starfish are rubbery, they need to be marinated for a year to be digestible. By the year-end, they will dissolve completely in the marinade, looking like globules of indiscernible meat. Best not to tell what the pickle is made of. People will happily consume when they're ignorant of its main ingredient. Tell them and they'll always be wary!

Remember to use ordinary starfish – brown with white spots, not the exotic variety – those taste yucky. A fisherwoman sits at the extreme end of the Mapuça fish market. She'll get you starfish if you request her. They get entangled in fishing nets and most fishermen throw them away. But I've persuaded her to get me some every Feb-March. Tell her you are Tara's friend and she will not overcharge. The two pickle jars on your doorstep are for you. Someone else almost opened them, but I saved them in the nick of time. Now I know why. It had to be you, Balgo, only you, who will open the pickle jar. So don't let anyone else do it – especially before its time.

Starfish pickling, in a paradise pond.
For you.

38

The Tara Salgaonkar Case

It's been a week since Tara's disappearance and the subsequent cancellation of her wedding. The humiliation was too much for Revati Salgaonkar, Tara's Aajji. She passed away last night, quilting her last kapiyaali. She was eighty-nine.

All of Saligao is expected to attend the funeral. Ramesh is being pressured by relatives to wait a day or two for the cremation in the hope that Tara will return on seeing the obituary ad in papers. But he sees no point in waiting. If Tara misses it, it's her loss; the price she pays for running away.

Tara's colleagues attend the cremation ceremony. So do Gregory and his family. While being worried about her safety, Ramesh cannot ignore the fact that both families have incurred heavy losses, the Figueiredos in particular. They spent a few lakhs on wedding decorations and a couple more renovating their house. Decorations and mattos were hastily pulled down the next day itself – the wedding decorator used them for another wedding.

"Mr Salgaonkar, police are complaining," says Gregory. "Asking for a better picture of Tara. I gave them a passport size photo from her Martins' ID card. That's too small."

"There was one on her dresser, Tara with her mother, haven't seen it lately. Rest all are pictures from school picnics and her swimming competitions… all old. Her colleagues might have a picture, a group photo or from a picnic."

"Tara didn't attend office picnics. In group photos, she's in a wetsuit, face covered or partially visible. I'll give them a detailed description of her features; let them do an artist's impression."

"Don't you have a picture?" Ramesh asks Gregory.

"Yes, but they're all the same," Gregory repeats, trying not to sound exasperated. "We divers wear wetsuits almost 24/7. I've rarely seen Tara in civvies."

Ramesh wonders if they went on dates in dive suits. He imagines two fully kitted divers framed by a restaurant window, periodically taking sips from their coffee cups, by lifting their breathing apparatus.

Gregory sighs. "I could never recognise her in civvies. Only when she came close – "

Ramesh interrupts, "Gregory, I need your help with Tara's aquariums. I'm feeding her starfish for the past one week. Suppose she doesn't return, even after a month? I don't know how to clean her tanks. I called a professional tank cleaner she had used once. He grumbled it was too much work and refused to come again. You know any aquarium shops that'll take them? Tara mentioned some in Panjim."

"I'll enquire tomorrow, Mr Salgaonkar. Let them be for now. They're the only things that can make her return. Tara was – is, quite attached to them." That gives Gregory an idea. Brightening up he says, "What if we put an ad saying her starfish are dying? Might work, no?"

Ramesh breaks down, "Forgive me, Gregory, for what Tara has done. But please leave her alone for some time. I know my daughter; chase her and she'll run further."

"How can I leave her alone? After all that we shared, I could kill her if I find her!"

Gregory is taken home by his parents. Embarrassments have become a way of life for them, this one more intense than Marcus and Clara – who it seems are destined to never return to Chorao.

The police give top priority to the Tara Salgaonkar case. The naval divers in a unanimous gesture pledge full support for search operations, if required. Tara was last seen leaving office for home, ruling out the possibility of an accident on the job. The only logical explanation is that she left for home, but headed elsewhere.

A team of detectives from Goa Police go to Bombay. They meet her old friends and visit her old haunts. But she hasn't kept in touch with any of them since moving to Goa. Her friends are clueless. As weeks pass, cops rule out foul play. There's not much that can be done, they say, if somebody decides to walk away. Children get lost; adults choose to disappear. Maybe Tara is hiding at some secluded resort, giving SCUBA lessons for a living. Her picture and CV are relayed to all beach resorts in the country. What if she has left the country? How many dive sites can one possibly search? How many coral reefs can one scan?

A month after her disappearance, Ramesh Salgaonkar shuts his orchard business temporarily. Renting his trees to another orchard owner, he joins the Ratnagiri Horticulture University as visiting faculty. He can no longer deal with the oppressive atmosphere at home. He locks the main house and the guest house, but keeps Tara's bedroom window open. He has stopped waiting though. Everyone has stopped waiting. And Tara's starfish?

He leaves them to die.

Eight months have passed since Tara's disappearance. It is no longer top of the news, nor is it priority for the police. Everyone has forgotten. Meanwhile, her father, Gregory, and her office colleagues have made peace with her decision to disappear.

Late on a Saturday night, the Calangute Police Station receives a phone call. A husky male voice talks nineteen to a dozen, without making any sense. The inspector on duty almost disconnects thinking it's a crank call. The caller, who refuses to divulge his name, says he has information on Tara's whereabouts. The inspector laughs.

In the last few months, umpteen callers have promised to deliver Tara to the police station. As if she were a gift-wrapped *mithai* box they looked forward to on Diwali. At this stage, what's most likely to show up will be in a body bag. But why speculate on that? When asked to visit the station to file a report, the caller disconnects the call.

A week later, a second call from the same husky-voiced caller pushes the police station into a tizzy. Worried it will mean reopening the case, they call Ramesh Salgaonkar in Ratnagiri, taking caution not to raise any expectations. Ramesh also hopes it's a prank. He has given up on Tara. Not keen on a closure, he prefers things stay open-ended. And, if she's dead, he doesn't want her body to be found. Dreading the prospect of being called to identify a body, he prays for the sea to swallow all evidence.

The caller does not rest. He insists that a close friend of Tara, who resides in the hippie dwelling, Casa de Paraíso, is behind her disappearance. He is hiding her. The caller begs the police to raid the Casa and rescue Tara from the hippies' clutches.

Ramesh immediately catches a train to Goa on receiving this information. He is optimistic for the first time in many months – and scared for Tara. There is a high chance she is under the influence of a hippie cult and their leader, Bholenath Guruji. Ramesh cannot believe she has returned to the vice den of a dirty old man who nearly ruined her life and pushed her mother to commit suicide.

How could she? And why? She had kept her promise and stopped attending his raves after her abortion incident… then why backtrack? Regardless, this is the best lead the police have had till now. Tara is alive! He begs the police to let him accompany their search party. Tara will surely reveal herself and return home if she sees her father's face. He needs to be at Casa de Paraiso as soon as possible.

And so they arrive, eight months after her disappearance: a pair of policemen in plainclothes, and Ramesh Salgaonkar.

Casa de Paraíso has changed tremendously since the older policeman visited nearly two decades ago. It used to be a notorious junkie hideout. All that changed when the musician-mystic, Bholenathji, purchased the property. Restoring the old mansion and the garden, he has turned it into a spiritual resort for artists and musicians. Residents practise yoga, paint, sculpt, and study Indian classical dance and music on its manicured lawns.

Bholenathji receives them at the gate. Ramesh can see why people fall under his spell. He too feels like prostrating, except that he knows better. The policemen are extremely courteous. Something about this man triggers a change in everyone's demeanour.

"Sorry to disturb, Bholenathji. Does Balgo live with you?"

"Yes."

"We'd like to question him."

"Regarding?"

"The Tara Salgaonkar case. Someone tipped us that Balgo has kept Tara here by force."

"Ridiculous accusation! People come here on their own. We don't force anybody."

"We're just doing our job, sir. We just want to ask him if he knows where Tara is. Is she here, Bholenathji?"

"Tara Salgaonkar? No! Both Balgo and I interacted with her just once, it was strictly professional. Two years ago."

"Can we meet Balgo? Just some mandatory questions."

"Told you everything there is, what else you want to know from him?"

"Sir, there's tremendous pressure on us to solve this case. We'll just speak to Balgo for a few minutes and be on our way."

"He's unwell," Bholenathji hesitates. "Won't be able to handle an interrogation."

"No interrogation, you stay with him throughout."

Bholenathji escorts them inside the Casa's sprawling property. People meditate on yoga mats under shady trees. Sitar, tabla and flute sounds waft from various rooms as they walk past. But Ramesh is surprised by the sheer variety of trees in the garden. He can usually tell a lot about a man by the trees he chooses to surround himself with.

Seeing the abundance of banyans, peepals, bamboos and rain forest trees, Ramesh is perplexed. This is not what he had expected of Bholenathji. This garden belongs to a nurturer, a life-sustainer. Not a rapist or a kidnapper.

"Balgo has his own house in Arpora. I got him here when I learnt of his illness," Bholenathji says, taking them to the servant quarter behind the Casa. Walking towards an open window, he points to a corner inside the room. A filthy, unkempt figure with matted hair is crouched over a piece of paper, drawing something with a lot of concentration. All around him, the room is littered with scraps of paper. The walls too are covered entirely with scraps of paper.

"He's an artist. Only Lord Shiva understands the masterpiece in his mind," Bholenathji says to the policemen.

"Looks mental," laughs the younger cop. "Tell him to talk to us."

"Stopped talking, since seven-eight months," replies Bholenathji.

"What? Why?"

"He has taken a vow of silence."

"Will he write?"

"He only draws, but I'll ask." Bholenathji starts pounding the door, pleading with Balgo to open it. He continues scribbling, oblivious to the racket.

"Let him be, why break his *tapasya*?"

The older cop snaps. Turning to Ramesh, he says, "See these hippies, they come here and throw our own jargon back at us." Smiling condescendingly at Bholenathji, he says, "Sir, how can you keep a mental person in your house? It's dangerous. Give us his passport and papers. His country's embassy must take responsibility now. Inform his family, process his papers and send him back home."

"No! Goa *is* Balgo's home. His papers are in order; his visa and passport are up-to-date. And he's not mentally retarded, just meditating."

"Does he go out?"

"Late at night, he takes his scooter and goes for two hours."

"Where?"

"Tried following once, but I got lost in the thick forest behind Saligao…"

"Saligao?"

"Or Pilerne, don't remember, it was late… "

"Bholenathji, we have to interrogate everybody present at the Casa right now."

The policemen line up all the occupants of the Casa – Indian and foreign. Showing them an artist's representation of Tara, they ask each one if they've seen her anywhere on the property. With no positive answers coming their way, they take the next step, a room-by-room search. A posse of policemen is called to help finish the task faster. Ramesh joins in as an observer. He's not allowed to touch any object. They turn the Casa upside down.

At first, looking for Tara, then, anything connected to her – her equipment, her clothes. After seven hours of thorough combing, they come up with naught. Ramesh is thoroughly dejected, and yet, strangely relieved that Bholenathji is in the clear.

The policemen apologise profusely, but Ramesh cannot hold his silence any longer. "Bholenathji, I am Ramesh Salgaonkar, Tara's father. I was hoping to find her here, but…"

Bholenathji gives him a hug. With tears in his eyes he says, "I'm so sorry, Mr Salgaonkar. Hope you find peace. Tara *is* in a better place. Wherever she is, she is happy at last…"

As they exit through the gardens of Casa de Paraíso, the senior cop notices an old Shiva temple on the far side of the lawn. He makes a detour to say a quick prayer. Some constables follow while some wait. Midway, he stops in his tracks.

Getting down on all fours he feels the ground, stands up and walks a few paces stamping the ground at every alternate step. "There's something underneath," he says to his men. "Call Bholenathji."

"Again?"

Bholenathji is summoned within minutes of being bid goodbye. He's not pleased.

"Why does this portion sound hollow?" the senior cop asks him.

"Oh, you're standing on a covered pond. It was extremely filthy, so we covered it with wooden planks. Weren't using it anyway…"

"Show us what's inside."

Bholenathji is stunned by the request. "Why?"

"My warrant says search entire property; anything suspicious needs to be looked at."

"It's a covered pond, for god's sake."

"Uncover it," replies the senior cop, nonchalantly.

"Too much trouble. I'll have to call labourers; it'll take time."

"We'll wait," says the cop, walking towards a Banyan tree. Leaning against it, he lights a cigarette. The younger cop stands between Ramesh and Bholenathji, unsure how to react to the sudden turn of events.

"For two days?" asks Bholenathji.

"Why not, it'll be a break for us. John, send the constables home. You and I will wait here."

"And Mr Ramesh?"

Looking at Ramesh, the senior cop says, "Mr Salgaonkar, please go home. We'll call you if there's anything. Take rest, it's been a long unsuccessful day. My sincere apologies."

Ramesh Salgaonkar decides to stay.

Five men turn up with spades and shovels. "Don't say I didn't warn you, it's quite filthy." Bholenathji laughs nervously.

After four hours of digging and shovelling, the labourers clear out a four feet thick layer of mud, stones and lawn from half the pond area. Thick wooden planks are visible below. The senior cop instructs them to cut a large hole in the planks.

"Don't understand why you're doing this. I'll have to spend more money covering it up again."

"You'll be reimbursed, Bholenathji. Are those steps?" he asks, shining a torch inside.

"Yes, twenty steps go down to the water."

"There's water in the pond? It's not dry?"

"Filthy stagnant water. It's dangerous, so we covered it."

The younger cop takes a torch and steps inside the opening. In a few seconds he scrambles out gasping for air.

"Let fresh air enter, then you inspect," Bholenathji reprimands him.

"Smells of a dead rat – lots of dead rats. Or lots of dead fish …"

"It's a pond, what did you expect?" Bholenathji laughs nervously.

The senior cop is unconvinced. "Let's call the experts. John, call Martins' Dredging, tell them to send divers."

"Why are you doing this? I'm a law-abiding citizen, my papers are in order. I'm living in Goa for four decades, but you're treating me like an outsider. Is it because I'm white?"

"We're just doing our job."

Chief Diver and Partner of Martin & Gregory's Dredging, Gregory Figueiredo, arrives to inspect the pond. He's surprised to see Ramesh Salgaonkar. They're seeing each other after six months. In the early days following Tara's disappearance, Gregory called Ramesh every week to check on him. Slowly the calls tapered, and then stopped altogether. Ramesh heard that he married a local girl from Chorao, chosen by his parents. After all that Tara put him through, it was a wise decision. Both men shake hands. Gregory looks happy and has put on some weight.

"So, what's it this time?" he asks the policemen. "Last time this pond made news, a hippie couple had drowned. Casa residents fished them out, and their embassies hushed the matter."

"Don't get alarmed Mr Figuerido, it's regarding the Tara Salgaonkar case."

That's when it dawns on Gregory, why Ramesh is there too, his face all ashen. Hoping that the pond has lots of dead fish. But not a *Tarafish*.

"But–but, how can she be – her body I mean – here? She never came here; she would've told me... she never mentioned... there's no record..."

The senior cop puts his arm around Gregory and reassures him, "Just a suspicion. Confirm it's not true and we'll all go home. Let's finish this for everybody's sake, shall we?"

As Gregory dons his wetsuit, Balgo – who's been watching all this while, suddenly becomes restless. He starts pulling at his dreadlocks and screaming.

Bholenathji drags him back to his room. He resists in spite of his emaciated frame, shouting, "Don't let them do it. Wait! Still four months left. Wait! Do not open the pickle jar! *The pickle will spoil!*"

Gregory walks down the twenty steps to the water. A tightly-stretched tarpaulin covers the pond surface. He cuts out a square large enough for him to enter. A noxious smell wafts out. Onlookers cover their noses and step away. Gregory has his breathing device, so he is oblivious. Diving inside, he slices through a blanket of fetid moss and water hyacinths. He doesn't have to search hard. Within minutes of pointing his torch in all directions, he sees a form at the far end, entangled in water hyacinths. As he swims closer, a vague indefinable fear envelops his gut.

Gliding with sparse movements, he is careful not to churn water. He frees the body from weeds, and flesh soft as cheese separates from its bones. Lustrous hair shine under his flashlight, like he's never seen it do before. He touches her curls – they come off in clumps in his hand. And then he notices something above her pelvic area… a tiny skeleton of a foetus. So tiny, he can barely believe his eyes. He adjusts his goggles and shines his torch to make sure.

As Gregory touches her lower back one last time, the starfish tattoo holds on stubbornly a few seconds more, and dissolves with the rest of her flesh in water, a skeletal Madonna with Child in his hands.

Gregory yanks the foetus from her womb and puts it in his pocket. He will give it the burial it deserves.

39

Setting Free the Hippies

Balgo is admitted to the psychiatric ward of GMC Bambolim and Bholenathji is locked in Aguada Central Jail. Goa Police is elated, the Tara Salgaonkar Case is finally solved. A hasty press conference is organised. It's official – the hippies did it.

"I don't know how her body landed there," Bholenathji repeats a hundredth time to the interrogating inspector.

"You sealed the pond!"

"I swear on Lord Shiva, I know nothing. Balgo sealed it."

"It's a bigger offence to aid and abet a crime."

"What crime? Can you prove that Balgo or I have killed her? Or put her in there?"

"Get a good lawyer to prove you haven't."

The anonymous caller wasn't playing a prank after all. Passing by Tara's house one night, he was surprised to see the lights on. Elated that she had returned, he entered her compound and peeped inside a window.

He saw Balgo, feeding her starfish. Had Tara sent him? Was she with him? Running as fast as he could, he stopped at a public booth and made the first call.

He calls again, after seeing the live telecast of the press conference. He blames the police for not acting faster. Had they searched the Casa immediately after his first call, Tara would've been alive today. The inspector informs him that the body's decomposition suggests she died much before his calls started. On being asked to reveal his identity and claim a reward, he flatly refuses.

"You know John, I think Bholenathji is innocent. The lunatic's done it."

"Absolutely sir. Balgo thinks he'll get immunity by pleading insanity. It's an American thing, I tell you."

"He's Australian."

"Same thing. These tactics work in the West, not here."

⚓

Protest marches spread across Goa like wildfire. This is the third dead body found in the same pond. Parents accompanied by children march to the Goa Tourism office.

"Drugs kill, as do drugged tourists," they shout. "Return Goa to Goans". "Make our beaches, rivers and ponds safe for our children". "No more Taras".

After two days of angry sloganeering, people run out of steam. Slowly, voices of reason make themselves heard. The earlier deaths were suicides, so the possibility of Tara's being one cannot be ruled out, they concur. Maybe the pond attracts depressive people, fascinating and luring them to death. Besides, wasn't Tara being forced into a marriage?

Press reporters and TV channels ask Ramesh for his opinion. He refutes the murder theory. "Why would anybody

kill my daughter? She was a loner; she lived and died for her work," he says. "I agree with the suicide theory. Her mother also committed suicide."

"Oh, it runs in the family," people conclude. *"But arrest the hippies anyway."*

After the din subsides, he reveals himself.

"Mr Salgaonkar, I watched out for her almost every night and day, hoping to stop her when the time came. Somehow she gave me the slip. Wish I had had the guts to hold her tight.

A shadow dancer
a tap-dancing tippler
Dancing among her trees
and her courtyard
with the shadows she cast
shining brilliantly for others
While he waited his turn

A note from the author

All the characters going berserk in this novel are a figment of my imagination. Any resemblance to people, living or dead, would just be a case of too many twins getting separated at the *zatras* and *zagors* in Goa. The roads, churches and the villages do exist, but their locations and their directions may have changed due to my inability to discern left from right at most times. There is no Martins' Dredging Pvt. Ltd. And no Casa de Paraíso, either. Paradiso, however, used to be a swinging nightclub on Anjuna cliff, till they shut it down. But it was no match for the 'Casa de Paraíso' in my mind. George Harrison is, well, George Harrison. May his soul rest in peace.

A RECIPE

I have not tried making a starfish pickle, yet. If you make one following Tara's recipe, do write to me and let me know how it tastes. To make amends for featuring a fictitious recipe, here is my favourite Prawn recipe for you!

Prawns in Green Curry

You will need the following ingredients:

- 500gms medium size Prawns (preferably white)
- ½ a coconut, grated
- 3 slit green chillies
- 2 medium onions, finely chopped
- 200 gm bunch of coriander (only leaves, no stems)
- 2 teaspoon ginger-garlic paste
- 10-12 black peppercons
- 1 teaspoon cumin seeds (or powder)
- 1 teaspoon coriander seeds (or powder)
- 1 inch ball of Tamarind, soaked in water
- Salt (to taste)
- 1 teaspoon jaggery powder or sugar
- 3 tablespoons coconut oil

For marinating prawns

- 2 tea spoons turmeric
- juice of 1 lemon

Method:

First, de vein the prawns. Don't throw away the shells. Instead, make a prawn broth by boiling them in water. Try and make about 200 ml.

In the meanwhile, marinate the prawns in ½ teaspoon salt, juice of 1 lemon and 2 teaspoons turmeric.

Make the green curry paste:

Use the mixer to grind your ingredients – coconut, chillies, coriander, pepper, cumin, coriander seeds, soaked tamarind. Instead of using plain water, add 100ml prawn broth (cooled down by now). You will get a smooth thick paste. Keep aside.

Putting it all together

Heat coconut oil in a deep frying pan. Add chopped onions and the ginger-garlic paste. Fry till onions are brown and the ginger-garlic loses its raw smell. Add the marinated prawn and mix quickly. Add the green curry paste, top up with remaining prawn broth. Add salt and jaggery to taste. Garnish with chopped coriander.

Serve with rice, Poi, Polas (rice dosa) or Sannas (like idlis)

The prawn broth is my magic ingredient. It adds more flavour to your curry. And you may use the shells as manure for your potted plants (only if they are outdoors). Or for your coconut trees.